"I do no... ...your permission to leave a room, Excellency,"

Lindsay told him. "Your servants might bow and scrape whenever you frown or twitch threateningly at them—they consider you their lord and master—but I . . . do not!"

She had a temper, Karim saw with some amusement, and when it was reflected in her eyes its fire made her more beautiful. Suddenly he had the urge to take her in his arms and kindle a fire of an entirely different composition, and the feeling spread through him until it was almost overpowering. Still, her effrontery continued to amaze him. It was a trait he found admirable, yet impossible for him to accept. No one—and particularly not a woman—spoke to him as she did. "But I am your employer, Lindsay, and in Cassar that's about equal to a lord and master, as you so quaintly put it."

Was he trying to intimidate her with that remark? After two weeks in the sheikh's palace she knew how powerful he was, but she'd die before admitting it to him.

"Well, don't hold your breath waiting for me to follow suit," she told him.

Dear Reader,

May... the month when flowers—and love—are in full bloom—especially here at Silhouette Romance. And as you know, spring is also that special time of year when a man's thoughts turn to love. Be they the boy next door or a handsome, mysterious stranger, our heroes are no exception! Six lucky heroines are about to find their dreams of happy-ever-after come true as once again, Silhouette Romance sweeps you away with heartwarming, poignant stories of love.

In the months to come, we'll be publishing romances by many of your all-time favorites, including Diana Palmer, Brittany Young and Annette Broadrick. And coming next month, Nora Roberts will launch her not-to-be-missed Calhoun Women Series with the June Silhouette Romance, *Courting Catherine*.

WRITTEN IN THE STARS is a very special event for 1991. Each month, we're proud to present a Silhouette Romance that focuses on the hero—and his astrological sign. May features the stubborn-but-loveable Taurus man. Our authors and editors have created this delightfully romantic series especially for you, the reader, and we'd love to hear what you think. After all, at Silhouette Romance, we take our readers' comments to heart!

Please write to us at Silhouette Romance
300 East 42nd Street
New York, New York
10017

We look forward to hearing from you!

Sincerely,

Valerie Susan Hayward
Senior Editor

LYNNE WILDING

The Sheikh

Silhouette Romance

Published by Silhouette Books New York

America's Publisher of Contemporary Romance

To the memory of
LORNA BRUCE-CLARKE.
My mother, my friend,
who believed in and always
encouraged me to strive, and
who lives on in my heart and memory.

SILHOUETTE BOOKS
300 E. 42nd St., New York, N.Y. 10017

THE SHEIKH

ISBN: 0-373-08793-4

First Silhouette Books printing May 1991

LYNNE WILDING

worked in advertising, was a professional singer and for eight years marketed romance books while nurturing, and working at, the dream of becoming a successful romance writer. She lives in Sydney, Australia, with her husband, John, and their two children. She loves to travel to distant places and, when time allows, enjoys reading, gardening and experimenting with exotic cuisine.

Glossary of Words and Phrases

abayas—loose garment

ahlan wa sahlan—welcome

dirham—unit of currency in the United Arab Emirates

infidel—one who does not accept the Muslim faith

jayyid—good

kaffiyeh—Arabic protective headgear against the sun

kaus—seasonal sandstorm

kismet—fate

massa' 'alkhayr—good evening

minaret—slender tower attached to a mosque from which the faithful are called to prayer

mosque—a Muslim temple

sabbah 'alkhayr—good morning

salam—a friendly greeting, a salute

shukran—thank you

souk—bazaar, marketplace

thawbs—long, loose garment

Chapter One

As the young woman shuffled forward in the queue toward the customs counter, pushing a loaded luggage trolley, she surveyed the scene around her and deliberated on the dubious joys of travel. El Hadjh Airport was small by international standards and bore little resemblance to the bustling Athens terminal where she'd had a three-hour stopover waiting for her connecting flight to Dubai, and then to Cassar.

Dark-skinned people, mostly men dressed in long, loose flowing *thawbs*, some bareheaded, others wearing turbans, milled around outside the barrier gates talking in low, animated murmurs. The air-conditioned airport was permeated with the distinctive aroma of Turkish cigarettes and the more subtle fragrances of spice and perfume.

How foreign it all was, she thought as she moved two paces closer to the customs officer. Smiling, she reminded herself that here in Cassar, capital of the smallest of the oil-rich Emirates, she was the foreigner. She handed her passport to the officer and was surprised when the man spoke in heavily accented but understandable English.

"Ahlan wa sahlan," he greeted her. "The purpose of your visit to Cassar, Miss Pentecost—is it business or pleasure?"

"Business," she answered his welcoming words crisply enough, while determinedly ignoring his curious stare. Then she realized that the uniformed officer's curiosity was aroused by her eye-catching Nordic coloring and the fact that she had traveled to Cassar unescorted.

"Enjoy your stay in our country, Miss Pentecost." He returned her passport and threw the automatic switch to open the exit gate.

"Thank heavens," she murmured sotto voce as she pushed the luggage trolley toward the exit sign. The initial excitement of gearing herself up for her new job was fading, as fatigue from the long flight from London invaded her limbs. What she was beginning to long for was a hot cup of tea, a bath and a bed. She had expected someone from the sheikh's staff to meet her here, and she scanned the throng expectantly. Finally, before a feeling of despair took over, she spotted a man holding up a cardboard sign with her name neatly printed on it.

She moved toward the tall, impeccably dressed young man. He was handsome, with his coffee-colored skin, almond-shaped eyes and tightly curled black hair. In his three-piece suit, which was cut in the latest style, he would have fitted into any trendy London office.

As she came abreast of him she slowed the trolley and spoke an Arabic greeting. *"Massa' 'alkhayr."*

He had been concentrating on the disembarking passengers and blinked with shock at being spoken to by her. Regaining his aplomb he replied courteously in English,

"Good evening. Welcome to Cassar," and returned his gaze to its original study.

His behavior made her mouth quirk impatiently at the corners, and she fought for his attention again. "Hey there, I'm the person you're waiting for." And she beamed a happy smile in his direction. "I'm Lindsay Pentecost," she said.

At that the young man—he was roughly the same age as she—looked goggle-eyed with disbelief. After a second or two of what could only be termed a stunned silence he recovered enough to mutter, "That cannot be. Lindsay Pentecost is a man."

A spontaneous laugh bubbled from her lips to echo above the general buzzing noise around them, and suddenly many pairs of dark eyes stared speculatively at her. Lindsay, realizing he needed convincing, opened her passport and stuck it squarely under his nose. "See! I'm sorry to disappoint you, Mr. Whoever-you-are, but there is no Mr. Pentecost, only a Miss." She mused half to herself, "Don't know how you could have got that wrong."

He pored over her passport details and checked her photograph, a deep frown crumpling his smooth forehead. "Oh dear..." he uttered. "Oh dear. This is most unexpected."

"I can see that." Lindsay's amused grin widened and she quipped in a clipped English accent, "I believe my father said something much more cryptic when he learned I wasn't the son he'd longed for."

"Forgive me. My manners, Miss Pentecost, they are atrocious. I am Shareel El Hareembi, nephew of the sheikh of the Morasqs. Er... His Excellency led me to believe I would be meeting an Englishman, but I am sure, after making your acquaintance, he will be pleased to welcome you to Shalima Palace." He took command of the trolley and began to push it toward the exit. "Please follow me, Miss Pentecost." Lindsay was happy to oblige.

As they drove from the airport terminal to the sheikh's residence in a chauffeured limousine, Shareel, seated beside the driver, kept her entertained with a nonstop commentary on the sights and sounds of the ancient city of Cassar. She was disappointed to see only glimpses of the city, whose mixture of old and new buildings, some clinging precariously to craggy, bleached cliffs, looked fascinating and would bear further investigation by her and her trusty camera.

All too soon they reached a set of heavy grille gates set in a high brick wall. The gates parted automatically as the car approached, and Lindsay, in the encroaching darkness, had only an impression of a paved drive, lush gardens with tall palms and a Moorish-style whitewashed building of huge proportions before Shareel ushered her from the car.

"His Excellency is anxious to meet you," he confided as they passed two impassive armed guards who opened wide ebony timber doors leading to a glass-roofed inner courtyard complete with a gently spraying fountain. All around were potted palms and a multitude of greenery including hanging pots bedecked with flowering plants, most of which were unfamiliar to her. The air was wonderfully cool, and she soon discovered why—it was air-conditioned. Her mind reeled briefly at the probable cost of such luxury until she remembered that the sheikh, with his oil and other business interests, was second in wealth to Emir Abdullah, Cassar's ruler.

Shareel pointed to an arched doorway on his left and said, "Perhaps you would care to refresh yourself before meeting the sheikh." Assuming she would, he held the door open wide for her.

In the elaborately appointed powder room Lindsay grimaced at her reflection in the mirror as she brushed the travel tangles from her wavy, shoulder length hair till it bounced and made an attractive frame for her heart-shaped face. Green eyes set wide apart and fringed by a mass of light brown lashes stared back at her. She observed for the umpteenth time that her nose was too pert, and the wide mouth below it with its full underlip was, more often than not according to her family, inclined toward stubbornness. She straightened her blouse, adjusted the gold chain around her neck and, with a resigned toss of her head because she could do no more, turned and rejoined the waiting Shareel.

Moving through another pair of carved doors they began to ascend a marble staircase. For the first time Lindsay acknowledged a twinge of nervousness at the prospect of meeting her new employer. What would he be like? How old was he? And then there were the children. What would her new charges be like? she wondered. The sheikh's last letter confirming her appointment had said there were three boys and one girl but, now that she thought about it, he had said little else about them. Oh well—her confidence bubbled to the surface again—if she had been able to control eighteen energetic fifth-graders at St. Justinian's Preparatory School for Young Men, how difficult could it be to handle four youngsters?

"One moment, Miss Pentecost." Shareel paused in front of an intricately carved arabesque door. "I will announce your arrival to His Excellency." He knocked, opened the door and disappeared inside.

As she waited to be summoned, the undeniable splendor of the palace became evident to her. She studied the decor around her and freely admitted that Sheikh El Hareembi had excellent taste. No expense had been spared in the decoration of the palace and the quality of the workmanship. And the placement of breathtakingly valuable paintings and artifacts was superb. She gravitated toward a hip-high marble column supporting a blue chinese vase. Was it Ming? she mused and arched an admiring eyebrow at it. And then, from behind the closed doors she heard noises that shattered the peaceful silence of the palace. They were loud, angry sounds—a man's voice raised in extreme displeasure over something.

Seconds later the door burst open and Shareel, wearing a clearly discomfited expression, beckoned her. "Please come. Er . . . His Excellency waits within."

Lindsay had little time to ponder the cause of the disagreement, but as it probably had nothing to do with her she instantly dismissed it and, seeing him waiting for her to precede him into the room, she did so.

Once inside she looked toward the man who was to be her employer for the next twelve months and, in the dimly lit room, saw only a tall masculine outline against the shuttered window. He stood with his back to them, seemingly unaware of their presence, and for several seconds she waited patiently to be acknowledged. Finally to quell her growing nervousness, she threw Shareel an imploring glance.

The young man cleared his throat noisily and said with deferential formality, "Excellency. Miss Pentecost."

At Shareel's introduction Karim El Hareembi spun round to face both nephew and newcomer. Instead of speaking, however, the temper he was having difficulty controlling temporarily rendered him speechless. Black eyes swept surreptitiously over the woman standing before him, his gaze noting everything. The Nordic coloring and attractiveness, the slender yet curvaceous figure, travel-rumpled clothes. But more than anything, it was the engaging smile spreading her mouth wide to reveal perfect teeth that succeeded in catching him off guard.

"Good evening, Excellency." Her soft tone sounded muted to her own ears as she fought to disguise what she felt at seeing the sheikh at close quarters. Handsome wasn't an accurate description of the man—his features were too sharp—but with his neatly trimmed beard, leonine crop of black wavy hair and his perceptive, penetrating stare, the effect on her was daunting. She had not expected the sheikh, a widower, to be so young. Her mind had pictured him being well into his forties with a comfortable paunch. But he was no more than thirty four and so...so... unexpectedly regal looking that her composure quite deserted her. She swallowed hard, suddenly tongue-tied, and stood there feeling incredibly foolish—waiting, hoping he would be the one to break the ice and speak first.

"Leave us, Shareel," his deep voice boomed crisply in a near flawless Oxford accent. "I'll call you later, when I'm finished with Miss Pentecost."

A fair eyebrow flickered upward at the last part of his sentence, which had an ominous ring to it. In a single, fleeting glance Lindsay—she was adept at gauging people's moods—sensed that something was very much amiss with the sheikh, and a tremor of anxiety began to take root. Maybe, just maybe, his lousy mood had something to do with her. But what? And more importantly, why?

"Now, Miss Pentecost, do sit down," Sheikh El Hareembi said. Stay calm, he commanded himself, though it was no easy task to accomplish. And then his mind wandered along a different track for a moment, deciding that the young woman's audaciousness matched her beauty. How dare she think she could perpetrate a fraud on him and get away with it? Didn't she know how powerful he was? Well, she soon would, and to her personal regret.

He pointed specifically to a hard-backed uncomfortable chair that looked as old as the Spanish Inquisition itself, and from his tone of controlled aggression Lindsay deemed it wise to comply even though she was nonplussed by his unenthusiastic welcome and obvious ire.

She sat down and tried not to appear self-conscious about her crumpled clothes, wishing, too late, that she'd worn a suit or a frock instead of her most comfortable skirt with the revealing side split. Arab men, she knew, had strict dress codes for women in their country.

He watched her settle herself, then moved to the desk. Leaning toward her he placed his hands flat on the desk blotter and said point-blank, "I take a very dim view of your blatant attempt to obtain employment with me by false pretenses, Miss Pentecost, and I assure you that your little scheme will not succeed."

And after dropping that bombshell, his hooded gaze dropped to the folder in front of him. Her name was written across the top, and he flipped it open to stare at the contents. In his anger, only the words he'd underlined on her résumé when he'd received it stood out: "teaching degree at grammar school level", "majored in languages—French, Arabic, fluent in reading and writing same", "excellent sports record—junior assistant to the sports master at St. Justinian's", "national finalist in college swimming team."

All of which seemed to attest, or had at the time, to the belief that Lindsay Pentecost's teaching credentials were first-class. He had made the mistake, natural under the circumstances, of presuming that the applicant for the position of tutor to his children was a male, and with a name like Lindsay Pentecost—so English and masculine—the possibility of *him* being otherwise simply hadn't entered his mind. She hadn't stated her sex on her résumé or in any correspondence.

Lindsay's eyes widened at his unprovoked attack, but quickly masking her shock, she found her voice. "Your Excellency, I have no idea what you mean by false pretenses." And, stirred by his hard-eyed stare and his rudeness, she added, "In fact, I'm rather offended by your suggestion that I have done something underhanded when I assure you I have done no such thing."

His black gaze narrowed, and for a moment he looked down his long, hawkish nose at her, subjecting her to an agonizingly long, silent scrutiny. And then he smiled a thin, knowing smile. "Impressive, Miss Pentecost. Your sincerity almost convinces me, but not quite."

What on earth is he on about? she wondered. His attitude and accusation made no sense to her. Also, the fact that he was practically calling her a liar had her temper, which was often hard to control, coming rapidly to a full head of steam. But somehow she managed to control herself and stare back at him just as coolly. "Please tell me what you think I have done."

"It's not so much what you've done, Miss Pentecost," he said, his lip curling derisively as he spoke her name, "but what you have failed to do. Failed to advise, that is. I was under the impression, an impression fostered by your application and your...unusual first name, that you were a male. Not—" his dark eyes flicked over her with dispassion "—a female."

Female. Lindsay's brows furrowed in consternation. What in heaven was he talking about? It certainly wasn't the answer she'd expected, and suddenly that and his attitude all seemed rather silly. Her lips twitched, threatening to smile as she asked, "And is the fact that I'm a woman a problem? I don't see why it should make any difference.

You advertised for a teacher, I applied, and you chose me. The fact that I'm a woman seems somewhat irrelevant, surely?"

Karim blinked and then stared at the young woman, taken aback that she had the temerity to almost smile and want to discuss the matter logically. She wasn't only breathtakingly beautiful, he deduced somewhat sourly, she bubbled with self-confidence and an uncommon sense of humor that at this particular moment was disconcerting.

"A female just isn't suitable to tutor my children."

"Why ever not?" she shot at him.

"My sons need firm control—" his eyebrow rose meaningfully at her "—male control and lots of discipline to prepare them for the rigors of an English boarding school—"

The words popped out of her mouth before she could stop them. "That is the most ridiculous thing I've ever heard." When she heard his sharp intake of breath she added a belated apology. "No disrespect intended, Excellency."

Uncharacteristically he chose to ignore her derisive outburst and continued on with what he'd intended. "Besides, you're Canadian, not English, and not what I wanted, Miss Pentecost. Not at all!"

What a charmer. As well as being an arrogant know-it-all, he was also a chauvinist, and her initial amusement turned to resentment. The sheikh wasn't being fair or sensible, but she had to admit that he wasn't the only male who had doubted her ability to control energetic, self-willed boys both in and out of the classroom.

She drew herself up straight in the infernally uncomfortable chair, which was a form of punishment in itself. "Let me set you straight on nationality. I'm English, but I spent my teenage years in Ontario with my mother, who's

Canadian—hence the accent, which I'm slowly losing," she added in a cool, businesslike tone. "My parents divorced when I was twelve. My mother was awarded custody and we went to Ontario to live. I attended Teachers College in London and after graduating I went to visit my paternal grandparents who live in Rye, which is in—"

"East Sussex," he cut across her explanation, advising her, "I spent a good deal of time in England myself."

"Oh." She barely acknowledged his words before continuing. "A teaching position became available at St. Justinian's, in Kent, and I took it."

"I see." Karim digested the background information she had given him with a barely perceptible nod and found, to his amazement, that his temper was beginning to wane, influenced by the air of self-assurance that seemed to emanate from this young woman.

With his intense gaze focused on her she knew how a bug under a microscope felt, and inside she surged with the determination to prove to this insufferable, supercilious Arab that she was more than equal to the task of tutoring three small boys and one girl. After her previous position it would be a piece of cake.

"For the past two years I've taught boys from the age of five to eleven and had no discipline problems worth mentioning, Your Excellency. Once they know who's boss— me—we get along famously."

"Yes, I'm sure," he said. "Still there is a difference, perhaps more than a cultural or racial one, between English schoolboys and my boys. My sons are—"

"Believe me, Excellency, boys are boys no matter what their nationality." She took pleasure in interrupting him again mainly because she sensed that he wasn't used to people doing it to him. He was an abrasive, inflexible man and so unfair that frustration began to well inside her. Why hadn't he specified in his advertisement that he wanted a male teacher, for heaven's sake? And another thing, why did he have something against women? But then the United Emirates in the Persian Gulf was male dominated—politically, economically and culturally. So perhaps it was too much to expect him to have any empathy toward equality of the sexes.

Suddenly she realized she was wasting her breath trying to persuade him to give her a chance of proving her capability. There was no way a man with his background would consider anything a woman said worthwhile. And so, heaving a barely audible sigh, she gave up. After all, she rationalized, if the sheikh didn't want to employ her she certainly couldn't force him to, especially in a place like Cassar.

Nor would she demean herself further by arguing her merits with such a horrid sexist. Let him give his precious position to a man. She couldn't care less. Wrong! Underneath she did care—a lot—and she was quietly furious. The sheikh had called her a liar, implied she was devious and assaulted her abilities, and what could she do about it? Nothing, except maybe steal a march on him and resign the position before he could terminate it.

She stood up, scraping the chair on the tiled floor as she did so, and with the high-pitched sound grating on her nerves she said, "Regardless of the fact that your ad said nothing about wanting a male and that you chose my application over everyone else's, you have made up your mind that I am unsuitable, and debating the matter further is pointless. I do not want—" she hesitated only an instant, her chin tilting proudly "—to stay where I am not wanted, so I release you from our contract." As she spoke she delved into her cavernous bag and brought out a long manila envelope and put it on his desk blotter.

Secretly she was pleased with her performance in front of this imperious man, but his unjust bias had battered her ego and brought all the old doubts about her ability to the surface. Not that she had any intention of letting him see that. "I would appreciate," she went on in a businesslike tone, "your arranging a return flight to London for me. And under the circumstances, I think it best if I stay at a hotel rather than impose on your... hospitality."

What hospitality? she asked herself, hoping he'd get her drift. She turned toward the door, painfully aware of his black eyes dissecting her inch by inch, but as escape was the foremost thought on her mind she blinked back a stormy tear and reached for the door's embossed brass handle.

"One moment, Miss Pentecost, I have not given you permission to leave."

The thunder in his voice stopped her as if she had run into a brick wall. She spun around to face him once more and said with mock formality, which was sarcastic in the extreme, "With respect, Excellency, as I am not in your employ I feel no need whatsoever to seek your permission to leave a room."

"Come back here and sit down. At once, Miss Pentecost. Or would you like me to come and fetch you back into the chair, myself?" He straightened, his hands drawn aggressively to his lean hips, his coal-black eyes daring her to disobey. "Lindsay Pentecost." He repeated her name thoughtfully and then proceeded to ask, "Who is responsible for giving a woman such an impossible, unfeminine name?"

Much to her inner surprise she returned to the chair, but in token defiance refused to sit on the uncomfortable thing. Instead she leaned her elbows on it and told him, "My father, actually, not that it's likely to be of any interest to you."

"Young woman, if I was not interested I wouldn't have bothered to ask," he returned sharply, his expression one of extreme annoyance.

Clearly the sheikh was accustomed to having his every word obeyed. And knowing she was the reason for his irritation she momentarily lost her confidence and said nothing. But then, seeing the expectant look in his eyes, she felt obliged to reveal further. "Unfortunately for me my father was expecting a son whom he had planned to name Lindsay after an archaeologist colleague he admired. When I arrived he was disappointed, but in deference to his friend he saddled me with the name anyway."

"How odd," the sheikh commented. "Didn't your mother object?"

Lindsay shrugged her shoulders. "She was very sick for a long time after I was born, too sick to be worried about my name. And by the time she'd recovered enough to be cross I'd been registered as Lindsay Marie Pentecost and was stuck with it."

"At least that explains your name, but how is it that you speak and write Arabic so fluently? Is it not most unusual for an Englishwoman?"

She had wondered if he'd be curious enough to ask about that. "I spent the first ten years of my life in Egypt, first in Cairo and then in Alexandria. My father was an archaeologist on loan to the Egyptian government. I attended a government school there, and later, when I was deciding on my majors for college I realized I had an affinity for languages. I'm equally fluent in French and can get by in Italian, too."

"Ah, yes, I recall you said as much in one of your letters." Karim's hands slid from his hips into his trouser pockets and for a brief moment he contemplated the young woman opposite him. She was direct as well as visually lovely, but the latter he considered more of a minus than a plus—the last thing he wanted was to be personally attracted to a woman employed to teach his children. And grudgingly, though he hated the idea of admitting it, she had been right about the job. Her application had been chosen over all others for the simple reason that hers was the one with the qualifications he had wanted. The only drawback was her gender. How would Darius, Ali, Hisham and Sonja respond to instruction by a woman? The thought of his eldest son's reaction to such a happening almost brought a smile to his lips. Possibly it would do Darius a world of good, he was such a little chauvinist.

"It's true that I was, er... annoyed to learn you were a woman," he confessed, and watched her eyebrows lift in surprise at the admission. "However, I am not an unfair man and I do not normally make hasty, ill-considered decisions. And I will not do so now. I would like to make you a proposition, Miss Pentecost."

Recognizing his conciliatory tone, Lindsay felt herself mellowing fractionally toward the sheikh, her body stiffening with anticipation. Was he going to suggest a compromise perhaps? One they could both live with?

"Would you agree to a one-month trial period to see how things work out? To see if you and the children can get along? If you do, then the position could be considered permanent."

That sounded reasonable, she decided, though she hadn't liked the way he'd emphasized the *if* in his sentence. She didn't particularly want to return to England and start job hunting again, or go to Ontario either. And from all he'd implied, teaching the sheikh's children would be a challenge. "Sounds like a reasonable deal to me, Excellency," she replied.

"Then it is settled," he said decisively, and in the time-honored tradition he held out his hand across the desk to shake hers.

Without hesitation Lindsay grasped the proffered hand, and with a sense of shock tried to tell herself that the slight electric tingle running up her arm was only her imagination. Absolute nonsense, she chided herself and made to dismiss it from her thoughts. But he was a dark, devilishly good-looking man, and seeing the fleeting speculative gleam in his eyes she knew that he, too, had felt the invisible current of attraction pass between them. Whoa there, girl, get things into the right perspective, she ordered herself. The sheikh might very well be the most handsome Arab she'd ever seen, but that was definitely all. Besides being a widower, with his wealth and position of importance as the second most powerful man in Cassar, there were probably hordes of eligible women of all nationalities eager for his company.

Not that she was interested anyway—in him or any man. Romantically speaking, the opposite sex was too dangerous and just too much trouble. She had been able to keep her heart intact for twenty-four years, and she had no intention of getting involved with anyone—especially not the sheikh.

Chapter Two

"**B**efore I call Shareel to show you to your quarters I feel I must warn you that my eldest son, Darius, considers all women quite unimportant creatures." He paused, his eyes appraising her again, then smiled at a private joke. Yes, let's see whether Miss Pentecost does indeed have sufficient intestinal fortitude to combat four aggressive youngsters. On appearances, and he knew he shouldn't judge by first impressions, she looked too soft—perhaps even fragile—to win a prolonged battle with his offspring. "Winning him over to your authority will be no small victory, of that you can be sure."

"You make him sound a real challenge, Excellency."

Her gaze moved away from his compelling stare and landed on the framed photo at the side of his desk. It was a family portrait showing a younger Sheikh Karim, the sheikha, and three children, one of them just a babe in his mother's arms. The sheikh's wife had been a beautiful woman. Dark, as one would expect, but with a dreamy soulfulness that was quite striking. Then the sound of his voice brought her attention back to him.

"They all are," Karim said with conviction. "I'm told Darius is just as I was at the same age, if I can believe what my older sister tells me."

"I see. And do I have your permission to discipline them in whatever way I see fit?"

He actually laughed aloud. "Of course. Short of beating them with a stick. Then again, maybe that's not such a bad idea."

She looked suitably horrified. "Excellency, I would never resort to such an action!" Then smiling conspiratorially at him, she added, "There are other ways to discipline a rebellious child, you know."

"I do not want to know how you achieve your results, Miss Pentecost—that you achieve them will be sufficient." He rose from the desk and walked around it toward her, saying, "I see you are fatigued from the flight, Miss—" He gazed down at her once more and a lengthening moment's silence engulfed them. "Miss Pentecost is so formal," he murmured.

"Isn't it just," she agreed, feeling her heart flutter erratically at his sudden closeness and the sound of his deep, masculine voice.

"May I call you Lindsay?"

"Of course. I...don't m-mind at all," she said softly, willing her pulses to behave.

"And you will call me Karim," he said authoritatively.

"Oh, no, Excellency, I don't think I could. It's much too...personal." She saw him frown and added politely, "I mean, you're my employer."

"Ah yes, but 'your Excellency' is quite a mouthful, too, is it not?" He was equally determined to have his way, and a silent play of wills took place between them. "I do insist,

Lindsay. But if it makes you more comfortable, only call me Karim in private. That's fair enough, isn't it?"

And when he smiled spontaneously and so winningly at her, she felt a most peculiar reaction in the pit of her stomach, and her thoughts scattered completely. With difficulty she swallowed the lump in her throat and heard her own capitulation. "All right."

On hearing his satisfied "good" she wondered whether she had just lost the first round with Sheikh Karim El Hareembi. That's nonsense, she told herself. He's only trying to make you feel welcome after his initial lack of hospitality. Don't read more into his manner than is really there. And you've read how charming Arab men can be, haven't you? Just about all her English friends had told her to be on her guard against their considerable Middle-Eastern charm. Thoughtfully she watched him lift the phone, press a red button and speak into the mouthpiece.

"Shareel, please come and escort Miss Pentecost to her quarters. And arrange for a dinner tray for her, as well. There is no need for her to dine with me and the children tonight, she is too tired. Formal introductions can be done tomorrow, at breakfast."

He certainly calls the shots, Lindsay thought, somewhat put out that he hadn't even bothered to ask if she wanted to meet her charges. His total control made her acknowledge that this was the way things worked in this part of the world. Men had all the say, and the women had practically none. And that difference in custom, more than anything else, would take some getting used to.

Shareel's prompt appearance and his delighted grin at the news that she would be staying dispersed her moment of pique at the sheikh's dismissing attitude. So she gave Karim El Hareembi the benefit of the doubt by deciding he was being considerate rather than autocratic.

"I'll hand you over to Shareel now, Lindsay," Karim said smoothly. "And if you have any needs he will organize them for you."

"Thank you." Then something that had been at the back of her mind came to the surface and she asked, "About the children—there are things I need to know."

"In your quarters you will find several folders," Karim said.

"Yes, they are up-to-date reports that I am sure you'll find comprehensive," Shareel put in with an accompanying smile.

"How efficient," she declared with a pleased, spontaneous smile at the sheikh.

"It was Shareel's idea, not mine," the sheikh told her. He was shocked at the leap of response he had to her smile. Why wasn't she a fifty-year-old bespectacled spinster instead of a young, vivacious woman? Her presence, he gloomily predicted, was probably going to cause havoc among the unattached male employees at the palace.

Bringing his thoughts into line, he directed his next remark to his nephew. "Once Lindsay is settled return here." As he watched her walk toward the door he turned back to his desk.

"Good night, Excellency," she called over her shoulder to him.

"Good evening," he replied dutifully, his hands already beginning to sort through the mass of paperwork strewn across the desktop.

But as soon as the door had closed behind them Karim's hands stilled. For several minutes he stared at the ornately carved door, a worried frown confirming his concern over the decision he had just made—to allow Lindsay Pentecost to stay. There was something special about her that unsettled him. Perhaps it was her special aura that stayed with him long after her physical presence had left the room. She was an achingly beautiful woman who seemed not at all aware of the fact. But then, she was no more lovely than many other women of his acquaintance.

Still, something about her struck a chord in the place reserved for Yasmin, his long-dead wife. There was no resemblance to Yasmin, yet, strangely, Lindsay stirred the embers of feelings...desire...a wanting to know the woman better—things that had been absent from his life for years. He sighed impatiently at his growing morose mood and tried to dismiss the Englishwoman from his thoughts, contrarily finding it difficult to do so.

He had chosen his future path and would not allow himself to stray from it: to devote himself to his children and to serving the Emir of Cassar in his ruler's dream to ready his subjects for the twenty-first century. And Lindsay Pentecost had no place in such plans, no place at all.

Lindsay and Shareel moved briskly along the landing toward another wing of the huge palace. As Shareel opened another beautifully embossed door he told her, "This wing houses the sleeping apartments. It was originally the quarters of the old emir's harem. The servants sleep on the ground floor."

"It's a magnificent palace," Lindsay enthused, not bothering to disguise her admiration. She had not seen such tasteful, understated opulence in one place before.

"Until the Royal Palace was built on ground overlooking the city, Shalima was the emir's residence. When Uncle Karim wed the emir's eldest daughter, Yasmin, the palace was given to them as a wedding present. Since that time my uncle has made many improvements."

"Then His Excellency has been a widower for some time?" With her curious streak Lindsay couldn't help asking.

"Yes, my aunt died five years ago, soon after Hisham was born."

"How sad for the children and the sheikh. She must have been quite young."

"Twenty-seven. Uncle Karim has grieved a long time. And since then he has buried himself in his work for the emir and in his children."

"I would have thought he'd be encouraged to remarry. Don't Muslims like large families?"

"They do," Shareel said, "but the El Hareembi family is not of that faith. You see, our maternal grandmother was French and she insisted on her deathbed that her descendants be brought up in a Christian faith—hers. The old sheikh—Karim is named for him—could deny her nothing so she got her way, as she usually did," he finished dryly.

"Oh," she murmured, digesting that piece of information with interest. She wanted to ask more about the sheikh and his family but didn't because she thought Shareel would think her nosy. In time she would get a complete profile of the man who was now her boss, and his children, too.

Shareel chattered on as they walked. "Emir Abdullah would like to see Uncle remarry for his own sake, and his children's, but so far he has resisted the impulse. Perhaps he has not found anyone capable of driving Yasmin from his memory, but—" he gave her a lopsided grin "—it is not for lack of female companionship when he desires it."

That came as no surprise to Lindsay. She well imagined that the sheikh, with his imposing looks and wealth, could choose any woman in or out of Cassar. "Will you tell me, Shareel, and please don't think I'm being morbidly inquisitive, but for the children's sake it could be important to know...." She watched him nod. "Yasmin, the sheikha, how did she die?"

"Ahhh, it was kismet. After Hisham's birth she wished to resume her career as an artist. She was quite talented. Uncle Karim did not approve—he thought she should be a full-time mother to their children as most other Arabian wives are. Yasmin and he began to argue, often, over the problem. One day—Hisham was just three months old— she and my uncle had a very heated argument. Yasmin was quite self-willed, you see, and according to the sheikh had been thoroughly spoiled by her father, the emir. After their quarrels, as was her habit, she had her favorite horse saddled and went riding down by the shore. When she was upset, the sight of the sand and the sea usually calmed her. When she failed to return after a couple of hours, Uncle Karim became alarmed and organized a search. They found her on the beach below a cliff. Evidently the horse had taken fright at something on the narrow path, bolted, and they had both fallen over the cliff to the sand below. The horse was dead and—"

"Yes..." Lindsay took a breath, realizing she had been unconsciously holding it in.

"Yasmin had injuries to the brain. She lapsed into a coma and never woke up, I'm afraid."

"That must have been a terrible blow to the sheikh?"

Shareel agreed with a nod of his head. "He blamed himself." And with a confidential glance at her added, "I believe he still does. But really, and even the emir agrees, it was just a most unfortunate accident."

"But the sheikh thinks that if they hadn't argued, if he'd let her have her way, she'd still be alive?" Lindsay asked intuitively.

"Yes. He rarely talks about her and no one at the palace mentions her name for fear of upsetting him."

"How terribly sad," Lindsay murmured. She was moved by the story of the sheikh's loss and said more to herself than to Shareel, "He must have loved her very much." And instantly she resolved to follow the palace staff's lead and not mention the sheikha's name in the sheikh's presence.

"Yes, it is a sad tale." He stopped in front of yet another carved door with an intricate pattern of flowers, vines and leaves, grasped the brass handle and thrust open the door, saying, "These are your quarters, Miss Pentecost."

"Please call me Lindsay, Shareel. 'Miss Pentecost' makes me feel like my maiden aunt who lives in Dover."

He seemed happy to oblige. "As you wish, Lindsay," he said and gestured for her to enter.

The room gave Lindsay the impression of coolness and light. Bed-sitter style, it was huge, and the furniture was also a pleasant surprise. Modern, with the exception of the wide, low bed which, in Arabic tradition was heaped with cushions of all different shapes, sizes and colors. The beige-painted walls and the solid design of the furniture had masculine overtones—it had obviously been intended for a man—but she would get used to that.

After showing her around her quarters, Shareel took his leave and Lindsay began to relax, at least she tried to. Her legs were feeling rubbery from the long day's travel and the confrontation with the sheikh. And so far, she conceded, nothing had gone as expected. But the biggest surprise of all—it made her head spin—was Sheikh Karim El Hareembi himself. No amount of imagination on her part could have prepared her for such a forceful, lethally attractive man, and as soon as her mind wandered in his direction her heartbeat became noticeably brisk. She tried to reroute her thoughts but that wasn't easy. He wasn't the only good-looking guy she'd ever seen, she told herself, but she couldn't recall anyone who had made as strong a first impression on her—ever.

An hour later she'd unpacked and had disposed of the meal brought to her by a shy female servant. She then took a leisurely bath in the lavishly appointed bathroom, toweling herself dry with a huge towel. And as she tied the cotton wrap around her slender waist, she was glad she had decided against bringing any synthetics to this hot, dry land where the daytime temperature could climb to 120 degrees Fahrenheit.

The large divan looked inviting, and stifling a yawn she moved toward it. With a brisk tug she pulled back the covers, eager to settle between what looked and felt like cream satin sheets. What a spoiler the sheikh was. Satin sheets no less, and then— "Eeekkk..." Somehow she silenced the scream as the flat, narrow head of a snake reared up at her, its beady eyes shining brightly in the glow from the bedroom lamp. Heart pounding, she willed herself not to scream—or faint, which was her second inclination. Beads of perspiration began collecting on her forehead and upper lip as she tried to control the panic within her. The poised stillness of the reptile chilled her to the bone. She froze and waited, knowing that any movement, however slight, could make the creature lunge at her.

And then she remembered a similar occurrence the week she'd come to St. Justinian's. Only then it had been a large, slimy toad! The ball of nausea choking her began to slip down her throat, but her gaze remained riveted on the thing in the bed. God, it looked real. Slowly she bent down and picked up her discarded slipper, and with some trepidation prodded the snake's head. There was no reaction. No fangs bared, no lunge, nothing. So, with a brave toss of her head she picked up the rubber imitation snake and looked it squarely in its fake, beady eyes.

"You—" her voice was a trembling whisper, her throat still tight from the effects of the fright "—have taken years off my life." Then abruptly she began to chuckle. "Those kids! They might be mischief-making little imps after all." What a welcoming committee they'd arranged, the little horrors.

With an unceremonious flick she thrust the rubber snake into an empty case. She pulled the sheet all the way down to make sure there were no more surprises, and with a relieved sigh she climbed into bed and closed her eyes.

Chapter Three

Promptly at 8:00 a.m. there was a gentle knock on the door. After a glance in the bathroom mirror to be assured that she didn't look schoolmarmish, Lindsay picked up her briefcase and opened the door.

"*SabaaH 'alkhayr*, Lindsay."

"Good morning, yourself, Shareel," she replied, closing the door behind her.

"You slept well?"

"Like the proverbial log."

"*Jayyid,*" he said approvingly. And with a meaningful glance informed her, "My uncle has told the children of your arrival."

"And, no doubt, that I'm a woman?" she queried matter of factly.

"Yes. Sonja is not too displeased, but the older boys! Well, I think you will have your hands full for a while."

She groaned. "I knew you were going to tell me that," she said with a sigh. "Guess I'll just have to exert my personality and win them over that way."

"If any woman can do it, somehow I feel that you can."

She smiled her thanks for the compliment and was still smiling when Sheikh Karim joined them in the tiled entrance. He wasn't smiling. In fact he looked decidedly grumpy, as if he'd had very little sleep.

She greeted him pleasantly with "Good morning, Excellency."

"Morning," he replied dourly and said, "I thought you might appreciate a peaceful breakfast, so I've sent the children to the classroom."

"I have already eaten," Shareel said to Lindsay, "but when you finish breakfast, ring the bell on the table and I will take you on a proper tour of the palace."

The sheikh studied his Rolex and then countermanded his nephew's suggestion. "I have some free time before my first appointment, so I'll show Lindsay around and introduce her to the children before we leave for the ministerial building." He then took Lindsay by the elbow, saying "The breakfast room is in here" and steered her toward a long, sunny room.

Sunlight flooded the room through wide glass windows that opened on to a terrazzo-tiled terrace. Beyond the terrace lay an expanse of lush lawn. Potted ferns and other indoor plants were placed decoratively in groups and, astonishingly, to Lindsay, made the room feel cooler. As in her quarters, the furniture here was modern—all chrome and glass. Against one wall was a long, timber-topped buffet on which stood several silver tureens and covered dishes. Another wall was comprised of floor-to-ceiling mirrors. The crystal chandelier, hanging low and centered over the table, should have looked out of place in the informal setting but, contrarily, it seemed to suit.

He pointed to the buffet and said, "Please, serve yourself."

Obediently she moved toward it. He followed and stood slightly behind her watching what she put on her plate. When he saw the single slice of toast, he commented, "I suggest you have more than that," and went on to explain. "Because of our climate we eat lightly in the middle of the day, then we do not eat again till after dusk when the air has cooled. I can assure you that one piece of toast will not sustain you till dinner."

"I don't usually eat much breakfast," she confessed and stared in amazement at the prodigious amount of food he was piling on his own plate. What an appetite the man must have!

"Watching your figure, no doubt."

His dry reply and the way his dark gaze slipped speculatively over her made her feel as stupidly self-conscious as a young girl. What was there about him that had the power to strip her of her confidence? "Not at all," she retorted defensively. "I'm just not hungry this early in the morning."

"Nevertheless, to please me you will eat a substantial breakfast."

He took her plate, and she was about to object to his high-handedness when he put in pertinently, "I don't want you fainting from hunger in front of the children, not the first day. It would give them a poor impression and they—" his eyes twinkled with wicked amusement "—would get too much enjoyment from such a thing happening."

Did he always have to have his own way? But she already knew the answer. Yes. In silence she allowed him to fill her plate, even though she had no idea how she was going to consume even half the contents. Then they sat down opposite each other at the long table and began to eat. Not surprisingly, she was overly conscious of the imposing man dressed casually in a pristine white linen thawb. Last night he had been against her staying and had only suggested the trial period out of some sense of fairness. Yet this morning he was trying to make her feel at ease. But his attempt at cordiality was having the exact opposite effect. She would have preferred him to be bristling with male antagonism—that image of the sheikh was more comfortable than today's deferential host. Was it perhaps his way of keeping her off balance? If so, it was a brilliant tactic... and it was working.

"Did you look at the children's reports last night or did you succumb to jet lag?" he asked out of the blue.

"I leafed through them, but I intend to do so again." She paused, then made the suggestion, "In a week or so, when I know them better, I'd like to discuss each child personally with you."

"A sound idea," he agreed with a nod of his leonine head. "Oh, by the way, only three of the children are mine. Ali is the son of my older brother. Ali and his mother, the widow Monna, have apartments in the far wing of the palace."

"That's a relief." She voiced the thought aloud before she could stop herself and, on seeing his puzzled frown, explained, "I couldn't understand why he bore no resemblance to you or the other children."

"He is the son of my late brother, Ali."

"Oh, I see, Excellency," she murmured. She looked directly at him and when his smile reprimanded her for her formality, she recalled last night's agreement. At once and for no good reason her pulses began an uncontrollable throbbing that slowly spread throughout her body even though she tried to suppress the sensation.

"It's Karim in private," he reminded her. "Did you forget, Lindsay?"

Pure reflex action made her apologize. "Sorry, I did." And get this into your head, too, Lindsay Pentecost, the man might be more charismatic than Omar Sharif, and younger, but he is just your employer and don't forget it.

"It has taken Ali some time to recover from his father's death," he told her, "but everyone at the palace has been kind, and he is now a healthy, happy child again."

"That's good," Lindsay said, knowing that at least she wouldn't have to deal with a traumatized child. She felt she'd have enough problems without that.

The sheikh chose an orange from a wide flat bowl in the middle of the table and efficiently peeled the skin till the flesh was revealed. In a complete change of topic he remarked to her, "I take it you had a rather different childhood, too, traveling around and then...your parents divorcing...."

"I guess it was unusual, but at the time I didn't think so. I remember some places, Alexandria and Crete especially, with affection. But after my parents' divorce my mother decided to return to Ontario where she had grown up. She went back to teaching, and after a few years she met a college professor, David Hatton. They fell in love and got married. The next year my half sister, Blaise, came along."

Another unusual name! But he made no comment on it other than to enquire, "And how old is Blaise now?"

"She'll be eight on Christmas Day."

He nodded as he absorbed the information. "And what became of your father? You said he was an archaeologist?" She nodded her head confirming the fact, and her long, loose blond tresses brushed her shoulders and swayed around to frame her face, capturing his attention for a diverting moment or two. Her hair was the color of the sand dunes at twilight; her eyes, in the benefit of daylight, were an arresting iridescent green; and her skin was creamed perfection that would, he was sure, turn to a milk-coffee tan when exposed to the Arabian sun. In truth she was a lovely distraction—one he did not need—and now he was honor bound to let her stay a month. That is if his energetic offspring didn't force her resignation sooner.

"Is your father still alive?"

Lindsay didn't answer straightaway. She was thinking about Harry Pentecost. Reserved, English to the core. He had never been close to her mainly because he chose not to be. The archaeological world had been his consuming passion, his only passion according to her mother, to the exclusion of all else. Finally she spoke. "No, he spent his last years in Israel working on several excavations. He died accidentally a year ago when several wall supports collapsed on him, and he was buried under the rubble. By the time they'd dug him out, he was dead."

"I am sorry," he said in a sober, sympathetic tone. "It is sad to lose a parent."

"Perhaps. It's hard for me to think of him as anyone other than my biological father. David, my stepfather, has been more of a real father than Harry Pentecost ever was." She couldn't keep the chill from her voice. The man who had helped give her life twenty-four years ago had, with his indifference, killed the childhood love she had once felt for him.

"But he was a respected archaeologist, was he not?" Karim asked as, thoughtfully, he watched her sugar her tea.

"He was," she replied, and suddenly the bitterness broke to the surface. "And maybe they should carve on his tombstone 'Here lies Harry Pentecost, Archaeologist Extraordinaire.'"

It didn't take too much sensitivity on his part to tune in to the bitter, disillusioned tone in her voice, and his dark eyebrows shot up in surprise and then settled again. Here was a marked contrast to the capable, confident woman he had met last night. It made him ponder over what her father had done to her to earn such enmity. "It's unfortunate that you think thus of him," he said. "And sad for your late father, too. He missed a lot in not seeing his daughter mature to womanhood and achieve her potential."

Unaccountably tears pricked her eyes, and angry with herself, she blinked them away. She had spent so many years, the first eighteen of her life, trying to win her father's approval and his attention—to no avail. He had been too wrapped up in his work to let anyone, even his own daughter, into his private sanctum, and that still hurt, sometimes unbearably. But what Karim had said had been totally unexpected and nice. He scarcely knew her, and he had just proved that within him lurked a sympathetic nature when he chose to release it.

"Thank you," she said, smiling briefly at him over the rim of her teacup.

"How did he fail as a father, Lindsay?"

She shrugged a slim shoulder, and her mouth tightened as memories swept over her. She could still recall vividly the few times when her father had praised her for a job well done, whether it had been academically or on the sports field, and how she had glowed with pleasure.

"He just wasn't interested in me, that's all. Maybe it would have been different if I'd been a boy." She paused, and after thinking added, "But occasionally he threw a few crumbs of encouragement my way, enough to make me determined to keep on trying."

He looked at her long and hard and then asked, "And why did you try so hard? To win his approval, perhaps?"

"At first, but as I got older I began to enjoy doing well."

"You must have been pressured, surely, to succeed? I mean, your father seems the type of man who would have expected that."

"Yes, but in the end it was a good thing. If I hadn't studied so hard I wouldn't have attained grades good enough to teach."

He wasn't really convinced by her defensive answer and with surprising intuition, for he scarcely knew the Englishwoman, he guessed that she did not like talking about or drawing attention to herself. She was, he deduced, a modest person indeed. An admirable trait in the fairer sex. So, with typical diplomacy, he changed tack and asked, "Did you join him on any of his digs?"

"Twice. Mother and I went on a winter dig to Abu Simbel and the next year, before I turned eleven, we went to Izmir."

"Did you enjoy them?"

She suddenly realized that Karim was subtly drawing her out, attempting to learn about her background, and for a moment, she was puzzled as to why he was doing it. She hadn't expected him to be curious about her as a person, only as his children's tutor, and that he wanted to know more sent a disturbing, though not unpleasant ripple of warmth through her.

Remembering those long-ago days, she smiled, in spite of the sadness they conjured up. "The first week was fun. The novelty of traveling, of roughing it, of riding camels and donkeys—and rubbing shoulders with his learned colleagues was interesting, too. They were a dry old bunch, but they made me feel grown-up. But then everything would settle into a routine and be boring. Usually we were away for two or three months, and by the time it was over Mother and I were pleased to go home to a few creature comforts.''

"Such as?'' he wanted to know, though he had a fair idea what she was going to say.

"Hot baths, clean sheets and a more varied diet, to name a few." She watched him grin at her heartfelt tone, and his smile reminded her how attractive he was when he wasn't being serious. Then she made herself gather her thoughts and continue. "It was in Izmir that I decided I didn't want to follow in his footsteps and be an archaeologist. I seemed to have enough sand in my clothes and sleeping equipment to last a lifetime."

"Your father made a fine contribution to archaeology. Last night, in my library, I found several reports written by him,'' Karim told her, and in fact he had spent many hours—more than he should have—reading them.

"True, but—'' She stopped, suddenly overwhelmed by a wave of bitterness she thought she had overcome.

"But what?'' he prompted, gazing at her tense expression.

"His obsession with archaeology ruined his marriage and for a time made my mother very unhappy,'' she said in a spontaneous outburst.

"Surely you exaggerate, Lindsay? You were but twelve when your parents divorced.''

The sheikh had no right to question her memory, she decided. And his continuing interest was both intrusive and unsettling. "It's no exaggeration,'' she stated firmly. She rarely spoke of her inner feelings, but now he had created the urge, and she wanted to continue. "Because there were just the two of us, Mother and I became unusually close.

And I know it took years for her to get over the divorce. Then David came along and—" She stopped mid-sentence, suddenly appalled by what she had revealed about herself and her family to a man she had known less than twenty-four hours. She had said too much, she realized, and the sheikh was too perceptive, having drawn her out without her initially being aware he was doing so. Well, she vowed, no more! "I'm sorry to be rattling on so, I don't usually," she said lamely and put her cup down so forcefully that it rattled against the saucer.

Karim prudently hid his delight at having been successful in breaking through her reserve. She had told him more than she'd intended, and that he was interested in learning more about her surprised him. Since Yasmin's death he had not been overly curious about any member of the opposite sex. So, what was it about this woman that stimulated him—apart from her exceptional looks and spirit? As yet, the answer eluded him.

"No apology is necessary," he assured her with a lordly wave of his hand. "I found it most—" he paused, his eyes glowing with an unholy, indefinable light "—enlightening. We consider it good medicine in our country to get such hostilities out of our system."

She regarded him dubiously for a moment, then put a question of her own to him. "You didn't major in psychology at Oxford, did you?"

He chuckled at that. "No. Mechanical engineering and political science." And sensing her discomfort he strove to make things easy for her by saying, "If you have finished breakfast perhaps we should take a quick Cook's tour of the palace and then—"

"The children," she finished with a soft laugh.

"I'm afraid so."

* * *

Lindsay and the sheikh spent the next half hour on a briskly paced guided tour of Shalima Palace, and by the end of it she was more impressed than she had been on her arrival the previous night. No expense had been spared, down to the smallest detail, with the unusual combination of some rooms being formally sumptuous while others had a really homey look to them.

The entire palace was a labyrinth of passages and rooms, some of which were padlocked because, as the sheikh explained, they'd not been used for years. Downstairs were several function rooms, offices, a huge library, a formal dining room, plus the servants quarters and the kitchen. And outside, though they didn't actually inspect it, was a long brick stable and exercise yard large enough to accommodate a dozen horses. Finally when Karim stopped again, they were back at the courtyard, and Lindsay, pleased to be able to catch her breath, had time to look admiringly at the fountain.

"I'm afraid we can put it off no longer," he said wryly, a twinkle in his liquid eyes. "It is time to meet the children."

She frowned disapprovingly at him. "You make them sound like little horrors."

"They are," he assured her with the authority of one who knows, "but quite lovable ones. Come..." He placed his hand under her elbow and together they walked down another, as yet unexplored corridor from which an unconscionable amount of noise was coming.

"Sounds like they're having fun," she murmured on hearing squeals and the sound of laughter getting louder as they got closer.

His only reply was a noncommittal, "Hmmm!"

Arriving at the classroom door, Karim opened it wide and almost collected a large satin cushion in the face. From that moment a deathly quiet fell over the large room as Lindsay, peering inside, caught the four youthful culprits in the midst of some roisterous game. Ali was piggybacking the smallest child, and Darius was pretending that his sister was a wheelbarrow. The whole room was a disaster area with pieces of furniture askew and other items thrown higgledy-piggledy all over the place.

"Darius, Sonja, Ali, Hisham. Stop this instant," the sheikh thundered, but the children had already done so on seeing the adults in the open doorway. "This—" his hand swept out, encompassing the room "—is a disgrace. How could you shame yourselves in front of your new tutor?"

There was no answer, and with varying expressions of guilt the children stood, ramrod straight and silent, fully expecting the tirade to continue. She put a restraining hand on the sheikh's sleeve and said, "It's all right, Excellency, really. Just some youthful high spirits." A swift look around told her that there was no serious damage, just a superficial mess, so she suggested to him, "Let's do the introductions, then they can use up the energy they seem to have to tidy the place up."

"Are you sure?" he queried with another angry glare at the children. When she nodded he turned and said to them, "During the day I will think up a suitable punishment for your behavior but now, children—" his tone became imperious as he tried to contain his annoyance with them "—come and meet your tutor."

Lindsay watched them approach, her experienced eyes assessing their pretended nonchalance. Darius's eyes were boldly defiant, his stance stiff with dislike. He would be a tough nut to crack, she guessed intuitively. Taking her lead from her twin, Sonja was also cool, and Ali's dark eyes were unfathomable. Hisham, the baby of the group, looked adorably shy and, from the liquid sheen in his eyes, was going to burst into tears if his father said another word.

"Children, this is your new tutor, Miss Pentecost. I expect you to greet her and to behave toward her in a manner befitting a respected member of the El Hareembi household." This instruction was intended for Darius, whose bristling hostility threatened to bubble over into a tempestuous outburst.

"Good morning, children," Lindsay said with just the right mix of warmth and authority. To get on top of this lot straightaway was a must or they'd make her life miserable.

"Good morning, Miss Pentecost," they chorused parrot fashion, and at Karim's insistence each shook her hand in a formal, if unenthusiastic gesture of greeting.

"Good, now hop to it and clean up this mess," Karim said.

"Why can't we get Hodda the maid to do it? Cleaning is her job," Darius asked his father.

"Not when you deliberately make a mess. You created it, now you can clean it up."

From the tone of Karim's voice they all knew the matter couldn't be debated. With a despondent sigh the four scurried about the room putting it to order and casting sly, curious glances at their teacher when they thought she wasn't looking.

The sheikh motioned Lindsay to follow him to the large desk near the blackboard, then said, "I can't understand what's got into them. They've never behaved this badly before."

They've never had a woman to teach them before, either, she thought, but to him, she said, "It's not unusual. They're just letting off steam and telling me that they're not going to let me take over too easily. I have to win their respect, and I fully intend to, starting now."

"That will do, children," she said suddenly. "You can tidy the remainder after we've had our first lesson. Please, sit where you usually do, and we'll begin to get to know each other." She watched Hisham promptly sit at the smallest desk, but the three others, as if by tacit agreement, took as long as they could before sitting down.

"Perhaps I should stay awhile," Karim murmured quietly to her. He was clearly troubled by his brood's behavior.

"There is no need, but if you would like to stay, then do," she told him, her heartbeat flagging as he moved to the side of the blackboard and leaned against the wall, his arms folded aggressively, his forehead puckered in a deep, disapproving frown.

"When I arrived last night I was disappointed not to meet you straightaway, but I was tired," she told them, doing her best to ignore Darius's bored expression. "However, I did appreciate the small thoughtful gift you left in my bed for me."

There was a small gasp from Sonja, and Darius promptly punched her arm. He appeared unrepentant and was undoubtedly the perpetrator of the fake snake plant. "I put it in a safe place and will always appreciate your thoughtfulness. I have also brought gifts for all of you. I believe to do so is a time-honored custom of your country. And at the end of today's lessons I will give them to you." She could almost hear their collective disappointed sigh at having to wait for their gifts, and she smiled inwardly. Perhaps there was a way to reach them after all.

"I hope you did not spend a lot of money on those gifts." Karim's tone was stern and hid the fact that he was impressed by her generosity.

She shook her head at him and then immediately had to fight the tightening muscles in her stomach. It happened whenever she looked at this arresting man. For someone who had made a practice of keeping men at bay, her preoccupation with the sheikh had a two-pronged effect on her. Her self-confidence zeroed out, and her pulse rate behaved shamefully, erratically, as if she'd just won a sprint in record-breaking time. To get her mind off him she thought of the presents upstairs. Before leaving England she had agonized over what to get them. After all, what could one give to children whose father was a megamillionaire? Still, soccer balls for the older boys, a brush and comb set for Sonja, and the wooden take-apart truck for Hisham were gifts she hoped they would enjoy.

"The gifts were thoughtful of Miss Pentecost and I hope you will thank her properly at the appropriate time." The sheikh directed his comment at the children, all of whom nodded gravely that they would.

Lindsay wished he would leave her to get on with the job. She could hardly tell him to leave, though, so she would do the next best thing—try to ignore him.

"Children, I'd like you to write a profile, a story about yourself, so that I might get to know you quickly."

Sonja's hand rose tentatively, and she asked shyly, "What do you want us to put in it, Miss Pentecost?"

"Your name and age, what school subject you like best and least, your favorite leisure activity, the foods you like, hobbies and anything else you feel you might want to tell me about yourself. Hisham," she spoke to the small boy, smiling as she did so, "I'd like you to draw me a big picture of your brother, sister and your cousin, using your colored crayons. Can you do that?" And when he nodded gravely that he could she gave him a big, beaming smile.

"Which language do you want us to write it in, Miss Pentecost?" Darius asked, his lip curling in a perceptible sneer as he accentuated the customary prefix. "English or Arabic?"

Hmmm... she thought. *This lad is going to take some handling. He has spirit, he's a natural leader like his father, and he clearly hates the idea of a woman telling him to do anything.* Getting him on her side, she realized, was going to take some doing.

"I assume your Arabic is flawless, Darius, and one of my tasks is to make your English as good. So, if you can manage to—" her green eyes locked with his in silent challenge "—write or print it in English. But if you can't, Arabic will be fine." For a moment she thought he would refuse to accede to her request, but after a couldn't-care-less shrug of his shoulders he dropped his head and began writing. Taking their cue from him, the other children followed suit.

Some minutes later Hisham said to his father, "Look, Papa, I have drawn everyone for Miss Pentecost." He couldn't quite get his tongue around her lengthy surname and it came out sounding like penguin, and the children sniggered.

"Excellency, I think all the children should call me Miss Lindsay," she ventured to the sheikh.

"As you wish," he agreed.

Karim's ready assent surprised her. She had expected him to insist on more formality and was secretly pleased that he hadn't. Perhaps it would help to break down the children's resentment if she was on an almost first-name basis with them.

Karim had been watching Lindsay, closely searching for a chink in her professional armor; something that would tell him if she could manage the fearsome four—Shareel's nickname for the brood. To his surprise and relief, she appeared not at all fazed by their misbehavior. She had taken it all with her cool, English aplomb. And so, he pondered, just maybe she could master them after all.

"I must be off now," Karim advised both tutor and students, ignoring the children's moan of disappointment. "Shareel is waiting for me and so is your grandfather, the emir." Karim nodded at his tall nephew waiting by the open doorway.

"Papa," Darius called, standing up respectfully to address him. "Will you return in time for us to ride in the desert this afternoon?" The tone in the boy's voice was noticeably wistful.

"I think so. If it is not too hot, we will," Karim said, and then he added a proviso that intimated he was well aware where the resistance to Lindsay's authority lay. "But only if your tutor tells me you have made amends for your shameful behavior this morning. And that you have worked hard at your lessons. You understand me, my son?"

The boy's shoulders squared as he looked his father in the eye and answered, "Yes, sir."

To say that she was mildly astonished by the sheikh's intervention on her behalf was an understatement. It was more than she had expected of him, especially after last night when he had spoken plainly of his doubts about her ability to succeed. It seemed he was a just man after all, and willing to put aside his prejudices to see whether she could make a go of it. *And I will,* she thought determinedly, her jaw pulling into a stubborn line.

"Come Shareel, let's go. The emir does not like to be kept waiting," Karim said, suddenly impatient to be on his way. He found himself needing to put some distance between himself and his children's tutor. She disturbed the

tranquillity of his thoughts far too much, and he had more
important matters to concentrate on.

"Coming, uncle," Shareel answered dutifully and, with
a sympathetic smile aimed at Lindsay, followed the sheikh
out of the classroom.

Chapter Four

Lindsay watched the sheikh, Darius and Ali ride off into the afternoon dusk for the third time that week and noted Sonja's disappointment—the girl was still too young to hide it. Lindsay decided that when the opportunity arose she would speak to the sheikh about how unfair it was to leave his daughter behind. Sonja had proudly shown Lindsay her own pony, Shalimar, and the accompanying tack. Yet it appeared she was never included in the all-male riding excursions, though she was as competent a rider as the two boys. Grossly unfair, Lindsay dubbed it, and saw the obvious favoritism as yet another example of the imbalance between Arabic men and women.

The opportunity to voice her opinion came that night after dinner when the children were ushered off to bed by Tima, the palace housekeeper. Usually Karim then retreated to his office to work, but tonight he seemed disinclined to and had asked her to join him for coffee in the comfortable private living room adjacent to the dining room.

Although Lindsay had been in the household two weeks to the day and was feeling more at home than she had on her arrival, this was her first opportunity to really talk to the sheikh. Conversations with him had been limited to brief polite exchanges over breakfast—when he was there—and when he joined her and the children at dinner. She would now have the chance to discuss several matters that had been on her mind. She only wished she'd thought to make a list. In spite of how foolish she knew it to be, whenever she was in the sheikh's presence he succeeded in disturbing her thoughts so much that complete mental coherency was impossible.

You're too old to have a schoolgirl crush on the man, she had told herself often enough, and she hoped she was too smart to let the feeling grow. Taking a deep breath, she turned the handle and opened the living room door. Instantly her gaze was drawn to Karim, and she wondered what he might think if he knew how her pulses were racing.

To combat the reaction she deliberately averted her gaze to the Salvador Dali painting adorning the western wall of the room, and in doing so encountered another man. Her eyes widened with surprise. The man, about twenty-eight, was only a few inches taller than she, of nuggety build and Arabic coloring.

Karim smiled and with a wave of his hand urged her to join them, saying, "Lindsay, I'd like you to meet Cassar's crown prince. Prince Zoltan, this is Lindsay Pentecost."

"Pleased to meet you, Lindsay. Karim's been telling me about you," he said to her with a charming accompanying smile.

Trying not to be overawed by the Cassarian royal smile, she quipped lightly, "Well, I hope it was pleasant."

"It was," he replied. "Karim says that in spite of the difficulties you're managing well."

She shrugged her shoulders lightly, and with a wry grin she confessed, "I consider the children more of a challenge than a handful."

The prince chuckled. "I must say that's an interesting way of putting it."

"Prince Zoltan is still a bachelor and has little experience with children," Karim informed her.

"That's not quite true, Karim. I do have several younger brothers and sisters," said the prince, and then added, "enough to make me cling to bachelorhood for as long as possible."

A maid brought in a tray and placed it on the marble coffee table. After she'd left, Lindsay asked, "Shall I pour?" to which Karim inclined his head in regal assent and went on discussing a business matter with Prince Zoltan.

Somehow Lindsay forced the nervous twitch from her hands as she poured the thick, syrupy coffee into three small cups. She was getting used to its strong taste and to the hot sweet tea most Cassarians seemed addicted to. In fact, she was even beginning to like both.

As she handed him his coffee the sheikh broke off the discussion to ask conversationally, "You were admiring the Dali as you came in, Lindsay?"

Not quite admiring it, she admitted silently, just using it as a concentration point. But aloud she said, "Yes, it's quite . . . imposing, isn't it?" Just like its owner!

"Personally, I don't care for it. Yasmin, my late wife, was the art expert. She studied at the Sorbonne and chose all the paintings for the palace, as well as supervised the decorating."

Lindsay caught the surprised look on the prince's face and surmised that it was unusual for the sheikh to talk about his wife. "Had she intended to paint seriously?" she found herself asking, curious to know something about the woman whose home she now resided in and encouraged by the fact that Karim had introduced the subject.

"She was quite talented but stopped studying when we married, though she continued to paint for pleasure. I built a studio here for her to work in." But it hadn't been enough, he knew. Yasmin had wanted more, and he'd denied her. She had felt that her creativity was being stifled and had longed to return to Paris and complete her studies after Hisham's birth. He had refused her permission and in doing so had lost her forever. The familiar sense of guilt flooded through him as he acknowledged that pride, foolish masculine pride, had influenced his decision all those years ago. He had thought it important to maintain his position as head of the household, to be the decision maker, and he had selfishly wanted to keep her at his side rather than allowing her the freedom to follow her chosen path. He sighed soundlessly, for with the benefit of hindsight he knew how different his decision would be today if she were still alive.

"I can't draw a recognizable cat myself so I envy anyone with artistic talent," Lindsay admitted.

"Me too," piped in Prince Zoltan.

With some effort Karim banished Yasmin from his thoughts and said to Lindsay, "But you are accomplished in other areas. You have your teaching diploma and you are excellent at sports." He turned to the prince and promptly disclosed, "Yesterday, just before sunset, from my office window I watched Lindsay in the garden playing soccer with Ali, Darius and Sonja. I was not aware that a grown woman could move so fast,'' he said, a hint of admiration in his voice.

Lindsay laughed self-consciously as she recalled the revealing short shorts and midriff top she'd worn for the game and realized she had unknowingly given him quite an eyeful. "Yes, but after ten minutes I was a lather of perspiration,'' she added meaningfully. "Besides, you'd move fast yourself if you had three active youngsters after the ball not caring whom or how they kicked to gain possession of it.''

"But you scored the only goal and won against the boys,'' Karim's praise continued.

"Still, I had an advantage, you know,'' she told both men.

"An advantage? What do you mean?'' Karim wanted to know, her statement having sparked his interest.

"I played attack wing in a ladies' soccer team in college,'' she owned up, her gaze retreating again from his handsome features and back to the painting. "We did reasonably well, too, reaching the U.K. college finals.''

The men looked at each other and smiled conspiratorially.

"Ah, perhaps,'' Karim mused, "it would not be wise to mention that. Let Darius and Ali think you are especially talented. The boys are mad about soccer and will respect your ability because of their devotion to the sport.''

That didn't sound quite honest, and she blinked her eyes in silent astonishment. "Even though I am a mere woman?''

There were chuckles from both men and Karim said, "Probably. Dreadful little chauvinists, aren't they?''

"Yes,'' she said without hesitation.

He smiled at her and admitted to himself that he was slowly getting used to her frankness in spite of the fact that, initially, that particular trait in his children's tutor had incensed him greatly. "Tell me, I am curious about this ladies' soccer team. How did one as slender as you survive such a rough, active sport?"

"I tried out for track and field at college, and though I didn't make the team, the coaches saw that I was naturally slim and fleet-footed. I was asked to play for the women's soccer team."

"And no doubt you did well with the young men in college, too, Lindsay?" the prince asked smoothly.

She shook her head emphatically. "I didn't date much. I had a reputation for studying. A compulsion to get distinctions in all subjects. That didn't make me overly popular with the opposite sex, unless they needed tutoring."

"It's hard to believe you weren't popular," Prince Zoltan said, shaking his head in disbelief, "with your looks and personality."

"I was a . . . late bloomer," she said quietly, feeling her cheeks warm at his compliment. She tried to steer the talk away from herself by saying to Karim, "That's enough about me. I really would like to talk about the children, Excellency, about my progress with them."

"I hope they are not proving too difficult, Lindsay?"

In spite of herself she smiled, remembering some of their more memorable escapades of the past two weeks, a couple of which had almost driven her to distraction. "I can handle whatever they dish out, and I think they're beginning to mellow . . ."

The phone rang, and Karim picked up the receiver. He spoke briefly in Arabic and then passed the phone over to Prince Zoltan. "It's for you."

With his gaze still on Lindsay the prince fired several questions at the caller, his expression serious. "I'll come straightaway," he said and then hung up. "Duty calls, I'm afraid. My father wishes to speak to me."

"Of course," the sheikh said politely. "I shall escort you to your car."

Prince Zoltan rose and his eyes mirrored delight when Lindsay respectfully rose, too. "Good night, Lindsay. I hope that we shall meet again soon."

"I hope so, too, Your Highness," she replied politely and didn't resume her seat until both men had left the room.

As Karim rejoined Lindsay in the living room his thoughts returned once more to Yasmin, but this time without the sense of guilt that normally accompanied them. Just talking casually about his late wife seemed to have eased the pain. And then he remembered what he had said to the tutor when he had subtly drawn her out on the subject of her parents' marriage. Perhaps he should take his own advice, and in doing so perhaps heal the wound inside him, the wound that kept him from being heartwhole.

Lindsay intuitively felt Karim's thoughts were elsewhere as he sipped his remaining coffee and wisely remained silent until he decided to break the quiet of the room.

Putting Yasmin out of his mind, he said, "I've not asked before because I wanted you to settle into the household, but now, are things to your satisfaction? Your quarters, the classroom facilities, the servants' attention?"

"Yes, I feel quite at home," she said. *Except when you unsettle me, as you always manage to do.* He had the disconcerting capacity to peel away the self-confidence it had taken her a lifetime to acquire.

"And the children's lessons—you wanted to talk about them. They are progressing as planned?"

"To varying degrees," she confirmed, wanting to be honest with him. As their father and her employer that was only fair. "Hisham is a delight to teach. He's such a placid child."

"And the others—the terrible trio?" he asked, waggling his eyebrows dramatically.

A smile dimpled her cheeks at his amusing description of them. When he grinned back disarmingly her heart lurched sideways for several seconds then, with much discipline, righted itself. "They're coming around," she said with perhaps a little more confidence than she felt. It was true about Sonja, but the boys—Darius and Ali—were still being difficult, still pushing her patience to the limit. She had to find a way to discipline their sly rebelliousness, if only to bring peace to the classroom.

"So you have no complaints, so to speak?"

His dark eyes lit with a disturbing intensity as they locked with hers, making her feel that only on the surface were they discussing commonplace matters. Underneath, his stare was probing her green depths, searching for something, she was sure—but what? Growing desperate to break the mesmeric effect, she latched on to his last remark and pushed the words through her tense throat muscles.

"Actually there is something I wanted to bring up with you." She watched him settle back in the chair and stretch his long legs out beneath the coffee table.

"Fire away," he murmured with that charming smile again, which quite demolished her concentration.

"Umm . . . yes." She waited for her scattered wits to regroup, worrying in the back of her mind that he somehow might know the effect he had on her. God, she hoped not. "As regards disciplining the older children? I'd like to know how far I can go with them."

"Go? What do you mean?" he asked, his forehead beetling in a frown which, with his hawkish good looks, made him appear quite devilish.

"I don't believe in corporal punishment . . ." she began.

"Neither do I."

"But, there are others ways of making a child behave . . ."

"Go on."

"By removing perks or privileges and using them as leverage to obtain results."

"Such as?" He watched as she flicked several stray locks of blond hair from her forehead, silently admiring the fact that she seemed genuinely unaware of what a natural beauty she was. He was not vain, but he knew that women usually found him attractive—all except Lindsay Pentecost. She seemed totally oblivious to his masculine charms. His gaze left her face to travel surreptitiously down the curve of her breast, lingering there for several moments before moving further down to her long shapely legs, which he had seen so much of yesterday. And he wondered if it would be interesting to make her conscious of him in a physical way. Suddenly, and in spite of his earlier reminiscence, the thought was tempting. For she had the air of someone unawakened by a strong physical emotion. But no, he checked the thought, such a liaison between them . . . to think of it was . . . insane.

"Extra schoolwork, or depriving them of the things they enjoy doing." She sought examples for him. "Swimming, playing soccer and special excursions and—" she paused, then plunged on "—riding in the desert with you."

His interested gaze bored into hers. "You consider that necessary? You might only increase their resentment."

Both of them knew she was referring to Darius, whose unrelenting resentment and lack of respect for Lindsay was making life in the classroom onerous for all. She shrugged her shoulders and said philosophically, "Either it works or it doesn't, and if it doesn't I might have to admit defeat."

A dark eyebrow shot up in disbelief. "Darius is causing that much trouble?"

"He's high-spirited and very male orientated," she told him, knowing precisely where Darius had inherited that particular trait.

"I'll talk to him," he immediately offered, suddenly and contrarily loath for her to admit defeat.

Her "No" was emphatic. "The discipline must come from me. He'll respect me even less if he thinks you have to back me up."

Hers was a bold decision, one that would either make or break her relationship with the children and ultimately determine whether she would remain in Cassar. He found himself silently applauding her for it, and he knew why. Lindsay Pentecost had interesting depths. She questioned, she was unafraid, intelligent and beautiful, too... a most intriguing person indeed. He sighed loudly and agreed, "You're right. I'll leave it to your judgment, Lindsay. So far you've done well under what must be trying circumstances."

"Thank you, Excellency." She saw his raised eyebrow and amended it. "*Karim*. But please, don't misunderstand me, I'm not complaining about Darius. Despite the behavior problem, I like him, and he's very bright. It's just that he's the leader, and if I win him over, the others will follow suit." She was pleased that the sheikh had aligned himself with her. She had half expected him to be smug about her having problems and encourage her to quit.

"Makes sense." He nodded, then with a sigh he heaved himself out of the comfortable seat. "I must get back to my paperwork now." He stretched his arms high above his head, an action that was catlike and full of sensual grace. "Our small state is becoming increasingly adept at manufacturing paperwork."

"Ummm...there is one more thing before you go, Karim," she said, an uncontrollable breathlessness in her voice that she hoped he wouldn't notice. She watched him turn toward her again, an eyebrow arched questioningly. "Why...is it that Sonja never rides with you and the boys?" She sensed rather than saw him stiffen and knew she'd accidentally hit a nerve but didn't know why.

He came back to where she stood now, towering above her from his great height and forcing her to crane her neck back to see him properly. "Did Sonja request that you ask me?"

"Good heavens, no! It's an observation of mine. I was curious, that's all, and it's obvious to me that she would like to accompany all of you." She noted the twitching muscle in his jaw and worried anew at the visible tension in him. Surely her question hadn't been that much out of line?

"Has no one told you the circumstances of my wife's death, Lindsay?"

Surprise made her blurt out, "Shareel did. And...I'm sorry, but I don't understand how it relates to Sonja."

"Sonja had nothing to do with her mother's death," Karim said coldly, "but indirectly I have been influenced by its circumstances."

Now it was her turn to cast him an enquiring look. So far nothing he'd said made sense, and she wanted to understand, very much, why he was suddenly all tied up in knots.

"Sonja is growing more like her mother every day, both in looks and in nature..."

"I've noticed the looks," she agreed, but he still hadn't answered her question.

"I've curtailed her riding because—"

As he spoke she cottoned on and finished for him, "You fear she might have an accident, too."

"Yes." The smile he rewarded her with for her perception had little warmth. "I have only one daughter and I do not want to lose her, too."

That she was surprised at him opening up was an understatement, and her heart went out to him in sympathy. That he was still badly affected by Yasmin's death was obvious, but she thought he was wrong in trying to shield Sonja. The girl, though she never complained, was feeling rejected because of her father's seeming favoritism toward her brother and cousin.

"I understand your reluctance to expose Sonja to danger but do you realize the odds of a similar accident befalling her? They would be astronomical."

"I do not need any mathematical projections to influence me where Sonja is concerned," he said stiffly, his previous benevolent mood doing a mercurial about-face.

"You're her parent and of course it's up to you, but I feel you should at least tell Sonja why you don't want her riding. She might understand then and not feel so left out," she persisted.

He marveled at her audacity. She was actually trying to tell him how to deal with his own children! This young woman certainly had nerve—more than her share, in fact. "You majored in child psychology, too?" He threw the question at her with a sardonic curl of his upper lip. "I think you should just do the job assigned you and let me worry about other matters. And I do not appreciate your implying that I favor Darius above her—it simply isn't true."

Isn't true! Was he wearing blinkers? Of course it was true. Stung by the feeling of injustice toward Sonja and his stinging tone, her chin lifted defiantly. She must be crazy thinking she could have an objective nonsexist discussion with the sheikh. In his own way he was as much of a chauvinist as Darius and Ali.

"Well, you sure fooled me, Excellency," she muttered tartly. "And your daughter, too." But deciding it was pointless to expound the matter further, she flounced past him toward the door.

"I have not given you leave to retire," he called imperiously after her and watched her spine stiffen with anger seconds before her tall, slender form pivoted around, hands on hips and her expressive green eyes blazing. She had a temper, he saw with some amusement, and when it was reflected in her eyes its fire made her more than beautiful. She looked magnificent, like an outraged tigress. Suddenly, and quite incredibly, he had the urge to take her in his arms and kindle a fire of an entirely different composition, and the feeling spread through him till it was almost overpowering.

"I do not need your permission to leave a room, Excellency. Your servants might bow and scrape whenever you frown or twitch threateningly at them—they consider you their lord and master—but . . . I . . . do . . . not."

Her effrontery continued to amaze him. It was a trait that was admirable yet impossible for him to accept. No one and particularly not a woman spoke to him as she did. "But I am your employer, Lindsay, and in Cassar that's about equal to a lord and master, as you so quaintly put it."

Was he trying to intimidate her with that remark? After two weeks she knew how powerful he was and deep down she was impressed, but she'd die before admitting it to him. "Well, don't hold your breath waiting for me to follow suit," she taunted. Then she made a rapid exit and beat a hasty retreat to the safety of her own quarters, her body aflame with temper, the blood in her veins surging at an accelerated pace. The man was impossible and...insufferable.

Twenty minutes under a lukewarm shower had cooled her temper, and she was in the middle of turning the satin covers down on the wide divan when she heard a discreet knock on her door. She tensed and glanced at her bedside clock. It was 10:30 p.m., and wondering who could be there she pulled on her cotton wrap and tied a bow at the waist before moving to open the door.

The sheikh stood squarely in the middle of the doorway, his width taking up almost half the open space, his expression inscrutable.

"I'm glad you have not yet retired," he said slowly. His senses took in her freshly scrubbed face devoid of make-up, and the faint pleasant fragrance emanating from her stirred his senses for the second time that evening. "I...this mail from Canada came for you today," he added, handing her three letters.

"Thank you." Her answer was cool, the memory of their recent verbal encounter still fresh in her mind. Perhaps he's come to apologize, she surmised, but knew it would be a one-off event if he did. Men in this part of the world usually didn't bother to apologize to a woman for anything—it tarnished their self-made macho image.

"Do you ride, Lindsay?" he asked out of the blue.

Swallowing her surprise, she found herself saying, "Yes, I used to go to my grandparents' farm for holidays—they had a couple of horses. But it's been a while since I've ridden."

"Possibly one day you will join Darius, Ali and me for a ride?"

Was that his way of trying to make amends for his earlier annoyance with her? she wondered. His version of the olive branch? If so, she would make use of the advantage. "And Sonja, too?"

His eyebrows jolted upward at her tenacity and then a slow, appreciative smile spread across his face. "Your persistence on Sonja's behalf is admirable, Lindsay Pentecost and . . ." He paused, deliberately lengthening the moment, his gaze riveted on her full, slightly parted lips, "Perhaps I could be persuaded." She apparently failed to get his meaning for her eyes lit up with pleasure.

Sonja would be pleased, and she was, too, but right now in front of him, Lindsay realized, it would not be prudent to gloat. "Thank you," she said, and respectfully lowered her eyes as she had seen the servants in the palace do.

"Good night, Lindsay," Karim said. He closed the door and walked down the corridor toward the next landing where his own apartments were, having to exert all his self-control to keep from laughing aloud at her mock servility to him.

She was anything but servile or docile, he continued to discover. In fact, she was a unique mixture of womanliness. Soft, fiery yet controlled and caring, as she had shown in her championing of Sonja's cause.

Alone in his long wide bed he sighed into the darkness and tried to rid himself of thoughts of the distracting blond woman he'd just left. Suddenly, his late wife's image came before him, and he pondered over the possibility that in thinking about Lindsay, he was being disloyal to Yasmin's memory.

She had been the sweet love of his youth. They had been betrothed as children in traditional Arabic custom and had grown to love each other long before they had wed. But he had been alone for five long years now and not once, until his children's new tutor had come along, had any woman stirred his interest.

Was it time to get on with the business of living, of being a complete man again? Was it time to stop burying himself in his work and using it as a means to keep his mind occupied and off the unhappiness associated with Yasmin's death?

There were no answers to the questions he asked. He sighed again and prayed for the oblivion of sleep to give him peace, which it finally did.

Chapter Five

Lindsay was in her quarters preparing the children's lessons for the next day when the telephone rang. "*Na'am*," he said into the mouthpiece.

"It is Karim, Lindsay."

His voice came through the receiver, its deep timbre causing a responsive vibration all the way down her spine— a sensation she could not control even though she tried. "Yes," she repeated.

"If you're not busy I would like to see you for a few minutes."

He had requested her presence only once before to meet Prince Zoltan, and suddenly she was filled with a sense of foreboding. Since their encounter in the living room and later in her quarters she thought he had been avoiding her. Now she was half sure she knew why. The trial period was over, and he was going to terminate her employment. Was he going to complain about her teaching methods, too? What, she mused moodily, was important enough to make him summon her? She glanced at the work in front of her, knowing it wouldn't take long to organize later and said, "No, I'm not busy."

"Good. By the pool then. The air there is pleasant at this time of the evening, and I will order refreshments. Coffee? Or would you prefer tea?"

"Tea, please."

Before stepping onto the patio, Lindsay found herself pausing to smooth down her skirt and check that her hair, which she'd allowed to fall loosely to her shoulders, was neat. Then she asked herself rather crossly why she was bothering. She wasn't out to impress him . . . or was she? Doubly annoyed by the disquieting knowledge that yes, she did want to look nice, she straightened up and proceeded to where he was seemingly contemplating the garden.

Looking up as he heard her sandals clopping on the tiles he said affably, "Ahhh, Lindsay, do sit down, the refreshments have just arrived. Perhaps you will do the honors?"

In silence she poured the tea and handed him his cup, after which she took the time to look around her. At night, with the pool illuminated by underwater lights, and with the discreet lighting of the garden, the outdoor area looked as modern as anything one might find in a current *House and Garden* magazine. So much for her ideas on uncomfortable, unsophisticated desert outposts. Clearly if one had money one could build or transport anything, anywhere.

"Tell me, how long have you been at Shalima now?"

She masked her surprise at his question, for surely he knew—right down to the day—and replied casually, "It will be four weeks tomorrow."

"I thought so." For a moment he rested his gaze on her composed features, noting how well the lemon skirt and blouse suited her coloring and that the tan she was slowly acquiring made her look radiantly healthy and twice as lovely to gaze at. And irritated with his meanderings, he redirected his concentration. "Time goes quickly, does it not?" he mused, not really expecting an answer from her. "You must tell me how you find the children now? In previous conversations I recall you said there were problems with Darius and Ali."

She arched a querying eyebrow at him. "Haven't you read the weekly reports I give Shareel?"

"Those. Oh, yes," he admitted quickly, "but I want you personally to tell me what you feel."

"I see." She was acutely aware of his liquid eyes, as black as the night itself, fixed on her, and she had to force herself not to fidget like a schoolchild. "Well, all the children have settled well." And with a slightly triumphant smile she added, "Even Darius."

"Yes, I thought he might come round once you threatened to forbid him to ride his cherished gelding, Midnight."

Her smile broadened. "He is quite bright, as I said before. But like many boys his age, concentrating for long periods of time isn't easy for him. Now Sonja..." She made to continue but stopped when he raised his hand to cut her off.

"We can discuss the other children at another time," he said dismissively. "I requested your presence because I...wanted to ask a favor of you." He watched her go very still and then lean forward in her chair, waiting for him to continue. "The Emir is having a formal dinner at the palace. It's in honor of some visiting oilmen and a U.S. senator. It's really a public relations exercise, nothing more, for our oil reserves are small compared to Kuwait's or Iran's. Naturally it is my duty to attend, and normally Monna, Ali's mother, accompanies me to such functions. But she is having too good a time with friends on a Mediterranean cruise and is unable to oblige.''

Lindsay had been curious about Ali's mother's whereabouts but hadn't felt venturesome enough to ask. Perhaps she was off husband hunting, Lindsay thought.

"So..." He paused, and his dark eyes subjected her to more of his hawkish scrutiny. "I would like you to accompany me."

She assimilated the invitation rather slowly but when it finally sank in her pulses began to flutter, then to race excitedly. Her response "Me?" came out in a squeak. "B-but I've never attended a state function. I couldn't. I w-wouldn't...know..." she stammered on, oddly overcome by the thought of being Karim's dinner partner and the importance of the occasion. "Besides," she finished lamely, "I've nothing suitable to wear."

At which Karim threw back his head and laughed so heartily that her eyes widened even more. "It's so like a woman to say such a thing," he remarked and then went on to assure her. "There are several fashionable boutiques in Cassar. I am sure you will find something suitable at one of them."

"But...I..." She stopped, realizing that she was reluctant not because she lacked something glamorous to wear, but because the tantalizing, yet awesome prospect of being Karim El Hareembi's, the Sheikh of the Morasqs', dinner date frankly terrified her.

"I've heard the boutiques are abominably expensive, but of course I will cover your expenses, whatever they might be."

Lindsay shook her blond tresses vigorously and negatively. "I couldn't let you do that. It wouldn't be proper. You pay a generous salary, more than enough for me to buy something nice to wear."

He smiled at her objection, knowing that she did not want to be under an obligation to him and found himself respecting her independence. This woman, he was learning, had many interesting facets to her nature. And with what he already knew about her, he was beginning to assemble a thorough mental dossier on the appealing Miss Pentecost.

"As you wish." Then, sensing she was about to belabor the point, he too leaned forward, his tone intimate and low. "Please. I would consider it a favor if you would help me out. You would get the chance to meet some important people—Arabs and Europeans who live here." He watched the questioning lift of her eyebrows and added, if a little slyly, "Besides, now you will want to make more acquaintances."

She ignored the barbed tone and queried, "I will?"

"But of course," he said with a casual shrug. "You will be staying on in Cassar as the children's tutor, and I assume you will want to make friends."

She failed to stifle her sharp intake of breath. Her gaze flew to his, shining with a delight she was unable to mask. Their eyes locked, and though they remained silent for only a moment, she felt something—she dared not name it— flow through her, warming and accentuating her already heightened awareness of Karim. He was too damned attractive and too potently male and proud of it for her ever to be comfortable in his presence. But, with some self-discipline, she brought her errant thoughts under control and smiled.

"The decision pleases you?" he asked, his voice noticeably husky.

"Yes. Of course." Though he hadn't said it in as many words, confirming her appointment was an admission that he had, in the beginning, jumped to the wrong conclusion

about her suitability to tutor his children. It pleased her to
acknowledge silently that she had won the children's trust
and even Darius's respect. And that was no small victory,
considering how difficult the frenetic, mischievous four of
them *had* been. And her triumph made her heart rate flutter all over the place again.

"The emir has expressed the desire to meet his grand-
children's teacher, too. So, you will accompany me, won't
you?" he pressed her again, his dark eyes daring her to argue.

Common sense and no small degree of self-preservation
told her she should make up some excuse to decline, and to
delay the moment of decision she asked, "What night is the
emir's function?"

"Sunday," he said in a clipped, formal tone.

A section of her heart plummeted while another part
soared with elation when she finally realized she could not,
and in fact did not want to refuse. "Yes, I'll be pleased to
go," she told him.

He clapped his hands together just once; a traditional
gesture for the completion of a deal. "Then it is settled. We
must leave for the palace at sunset on Sunday."

He was clearly pleased that she had said yes. That he
would seek her company on a social occasion somewhat
surprised her, for she was certain that he didn't lack female company in Cassar. She just hoped she would not
goof in front of any VIPs who would be there. She would
die of embarrassment if she inadvertently breached proto-
col.

He put down his empty teacup, and with a sigh he murmured, "And now I must get back to work." Yet he felt
oddly reluctant, he admitted to himself, to quit the tran-
quil garden and Lindsay's delightful company. But after a

few more pleasantries, which he stretched out for ten minutes, he took his leave.

Lindsay stood in front of the tall, mirrored wardrobe door. She turned to the side, then straight on, and then repeated the maneuver. Though she had at first almost fainted at the inflated price tag, the apple-green, gossamer, full-length gown now seemed worth it. It fitted perfectly and made her look so chic.

Tonight she would be meeting oil magnates, a few diplomats, wealthy Arab businessmen and others. Shareel had filled her in on the expected guest list and she didn't want to let Karim down by not looking the part. She picked up the matching leather purse, and with a final settling pat of her hair, which was swept up in a chignon for the occasion, left her quarters.

As she descended the staircase she thought she heard voices—Shareel's and Karim's. They were at the fountain in the courtyard talking animatedly, and when her eyes fastened on Karim she almost lost her footing and tripped. He was dressed formally in white eastern-style clothes, and he looked so virile and handsome that involuntarily Lindsay's stomach muscles did a series of acrobatic moves, and her throat tightened till it was almost painful.

A premonition shivered down her spine that, after tonight, no matter how the evening went, things would not be the same. Karim El Hareembi, First Minister of Cassar, was dismantling the barbed-wire fence she had put around her heart—an imaginary but very real barrier she had placed there to prevent her emotions from taking over. And the strength of what she was beginning to feel frightened her witless. She would have to control these unruly emotions of hers. Somehow . . . some way.

Shareel turned, watched her descend to the bottom of the stairs and said, "Lindsay, you look sensational," and sought the sheikh's confirmation. "Doesn't she, Uncle?"

There was an imperceptible silence before Karim answered, "Yes." And when her green eyes widened spontaneously with pleasure and she smiled, he smiled back. Lindsay and Yasmin were as dissimilar as night and day, yet the Englishwoman was beginning to dominate his thoughts and stir feelings he thought had died with his wife's passing. "I fear I will spend half the evening keeping those amorous oilmen away from her," he teased lightly to mask the fact that he was affected by her beauty.

She was quick to assure both men, "I'm not a child in need of protection. I'm quite capable of handling men." Her eyes sparkled, daring Karim to challenge her words. "Oilmen or any other kind."

Karim laughed heartily and nodded approvingly. "Yes, Lindsay Pentecost, I do believe you're a match for anyone. Come..."

He placed his hand on the small of her back. She felt the warmth of his touch torch through the filmy material to her skin, and goose bumps erupted instantly. She gave a little quiver and hoped he wouldn't notice, but he did.

"You are cold? Or..." he enquired looking down at her, his eyes aglow with something indefinable, "just nervous?"

"Neither." She tossed the suggestion off and tried to muster some control over her erratic pulse rate. "It was just one of those walking-over-your-grave shivers." But his deferential "I see" sounded unconvinced, and she bit her lip with irritation, trying to regain total composure.

They said goodbye to Shareel, and Karim, his hand steadfastly on her back, guided her to the waiting limousine. He saw her settled before climbing into the back to sit beside her.

Suddenly, though the interior of the car was spacious, the closeness between them caused Lindsay's latent self-consciousness to surface, a feeling only he could kindle in her.

Watching her fingers pluck aimlessly at imaginary threads on her lap, Karim, in a low intimate tone he rarely used, asked, "Sure you're not nervous, Lindsay?"

"A little," she had to admit. But her nerves were caused more by close proximity to him than by meeting a roomful of strangers, though naturally she couldn't tell him that.

"There's no need," he assured her. "The way you look tonight, all will be impressed with your youth and beauty, believe me."

He had said she was beautiful...and that admission from him threw her thoughts all over the place for the rest of the journey.

Emir Abdullah of Cassar's palace was twice the size of Shalima Palace. As they walked up the marble steps covered in red carpet for the occasion, Lindsay commanded herself not to gape like an overawed tourist. But still, the sight of huge, turbaned black guards with oiled bare torsos and baggy pants holding broad, gleaming scimitars across their chests was dramatic, to say the least, like a scene from an exotic Hollywood movie.

Karim saw her eyeing the guards and bent his head to whisper, "They're purely for show, for the Westerners. The emir enjoys his little theatrics and uses them to keep businessmen off guard. It's amazing how amenable some of them become when they are confronted by scimitar-wielding guards."

"He sounds like a cunning old devil to me," she whispered back, momentarily forgetting that Karim was the ruler's son-in-law.

"You'll find out soon enough" was all her dinner date would say on that score.

The butterflies in her stomach—the ones she thought had gone to sleep—awoke and began to rampage about, and she found herself tightening her grip on his arm.

The din of many voices talking at once could be heard plainly as they approached two huge brass-embossed doors. When they were closer, two palace servants, suitably attired in silk and heavily braided uniforms, pulled the giant handles, and the doors swung open to reveal the palace's reception room.

Then came a turbaned majordomo's formal announcement. "Sheikh Karim El Hareembi, First Minister of Cassar, and . . . Miss Lindsay Pentecost."

The babbling hum lulled for an instant, then resumed as the first minister and his companion walked down the carpeted steps into the throng where they were immediately engulfed by a wave of people wanting to meet both of them.

Meeting the emir was not the ordeal Lindsay thought it would be. He was a roly-poly, benevolent-looking man, well into middle age, and he was positively charming and welcomed her effusively to his small state.

"The pleasure is all mine, Your Highness," she said in Arabic. Normally she would have returned the emir's curious stare—she used that technique when the traders and the spice merchants at the souk appraised her as if she were a piece of meat on a slab. But in deference to his being the ruler—in Cassar he was the law—she gave a small curtsy and lowered her eyes respectfully as she had seen Karim's servants do when he spoke to them.

"It is a pleasure to meet you at last, Miss Pentecost...Lindsay. I see that Shareel El Hareembi's and my son's descriptions of you were accurate," Emir Abdullah replied in accented English. Turning to Karim he remarked, "I see why the townspeople call her *blanc infidèl*, too." His beringed hand reached out to tilt up her chin so he could see into her eyes. "Eyes like emeralds. They are magnificent, are they not, Karim? And so demure..."

But Karim could not control the need to refute that assessment and murmured confidentially, "Miss Pentecost is many things, oh Lord of Cassar—an excellent teacher, an admirable sportswoman and according to my children she also sings like an angel. But demure, Highness, she definitely is not!"

Outraged and more than a little embarrassed by the sheikh's frankness she uttered a shocked "Excellency!" her eyes flashing fire while she struggled to stop her cheeks from turning a fiery red.

"Ah, yes, I see it—the fire you spoke of before," the emir said to Karim. "*Jayyid,* I like a woman with spirit. Come," he said, taking her hand and linking it through his arm. "We shall meet my guests together. I want to watch the women's eyes when they confront your loveliness."

He is an old rogue, Lindsay decided as they moved away from the sheikh. Something of her opinion must have been betrayed in her expression for the emir gave her a wicked grin and squeezed her arm.

"The first minister was correct, my dear—subservience is quite alien to you." And then with regal prerogative he changed the subject. "You must tell me about Yasmin's children. Young Darius is a handful, is he not?"

She half turned back to look at Karim who shrugged his shoulders and waved her a subtle goodbye. "I am pleased to report," she told Cassar's ruler, "that Darius and I have reached an understanding."

"You mean a truce?" he interpreted, punctuating it with a deep chuckle.

She laughed, too, and confessed, "Something like that . . ."

Dinner was served in an incredibly large room decorated with an abundance of Turkish wall hangings and all manner of works of art—a real showcase of the emir's immense wealth. Lindsay thought the meal would be served Western-style, as in Karim's home, but here the guests were seated on colorful cushions around low tables, and several courses of spicy, mouth-watering food were served to them on huge platters by a continuing stream of liveried servants. There were sauces to dip meat and flat bread into, and only a thin, sharp dagger with which to spear or cut the food. It was different from anything she had ever experienced, and sitting diagonally opposite Karim, she intercepted several glances from him. His expressive dark eyes were saying as eloquently as words that she was holding her own in the company of Arab princes, oil barons and diplomats.

She was very much aware of the man across the table—his potent attractiveness kept her physical and emotional sensors at a high level of alertness. He stood out prominently among the other men, having a special dark, Eastern charisma that drew men and women to him—especially the latter. Several European women had already made their preference for his company embarrassingly obvious and given her looks that could kill. But that he appeared to respond and bask in their adulation without being overly impressed by it came as no surprise to Lindsay. Karim El Hareembi was a level-headed man who knew precisely where he was going and had sublime confidence in his exceptional ability.

After the lengthy dinner and welcoming speeches there was entertainment in a formal salon-style ballroom, but this time Karim made sure they sat side by side. Two belly dancers, youthful yet curvaceous, came onto the cleared space accompanied by three musicians, and the music and the dancers' gyrations provided the guests with rare entertainment.

Karim leaned toward her and asked in an undertone, "You are enjoying the evening, Lindsay?" But his question was superfluous, he soon realized, as the ready smile she gave him was an answer in itself.

"Oh, yes, everyone has been so friendly."

"Good." He was pleased. "And I notice you have won at least two hearts tonight." At his remark she laughed low in her throat and the unconscious sexiness of the sound made his stare suddenly more intense. She looked positively radiant; her warm personality, when she wasn't upset about something, shone through. It made him realize somewhat belatedly that he had been remiss in not introducing her to the emir and Cassarian society before tonight.

"Only two?" she queried with a mock pout. "I was hoping for at least three, maybe four."

He smiled back indulgently, silently amazed by her metamorphosis. Tonight she was so vibrant, like someone who had only just discovered her full potential. A part of him— the selfish, masculine part of him—somehow regretted that he had been the catalyst of such a blossoming. From now on she would not lack companionship, especially from men, when her duties for the day as the children's tutor were over. "Well, maybe three then," he said in a jovial yet intimate tone.

Their eyes met, and Lindsay glimpsed something in his dark depths—just for a second—before they became hooded. She had seen desire there, and for a moment its impact robbed her of breath, of thought, of will. Something was happening to them both that was beyond her ability to stop, and the strength of the embryonic feeling alarmed her. She gulped in a deep, calming breath. Had she really seen what she thought? Or was her imagination, stimulated by the romance of the evening, playing her for a fool. No, she told herself, she would not think about that look in Karim's eyes. But already her limbs had softened to jelly, and there was a singing, a coursing, through her veins that made denial of her reaction foolish.

She would fight such feelings, she vowed. She must, because such an attraction was dangerous to her sanity, and she had decided long ago, after an unsatisfactory relationship while in college, to steer clear of romantic commitments. And with the sheikh it could only lead to heartbreak . . . hers.

Chapter Six

After the entertainment a new band of musicians came in, and an area was cleared for guests to dance if they so desired. Servants took around small cups of strong, black coffee and sweetened honey cakes. After the sumptuous feast they'd all so recently indulged in, Lindsay doubted her stomach's capacity to take another ounce.

"The emir has especially requested I give you a tour of his water garden. Everyone in Cassar knows how proud he is of it," Karim said to her.

"Oh, yes, do. It would be lovely," she replied, secretly delighted to be able to exercise off the effects of the dinner.

With Karim's guiding hand at Lindsay's elbow they reached the patio where a number of oil-lit lanterns gave a soft glow to the granite slab floor. The night air was cool and quiet, a pleasant change from the palace where the noisy chatter of a hundred people and the mushrooming cloud of cigarette smoke were becoming oppressive. They began to wander down one of the gravel paths. Manicured hedges grew on both sides and the air was heavy with the perfume of some night-blooming flowers. As they walked he explained that the water garden, though a scaled-down version, had been modelled after one at Tivoli, near Rome. The emir had once visited it and become enchanted by its unique aqua-engineering and beauty.

In a leafy bower, Karim turned to her. "In truth, Lindsay, my real motive in showing you the garden was a selfish one," he said. She stared at him nonplussed until he explained. "An executive from an American consortium has been pressing me for days—he wants to discuss increasing our oil production. He probably thought he could corner me here tonight and possibly get the answer he wants."

"So what has that got to do with us viewing the garden?" she wanted to know.

"Well, he would hardly follow me into the garden to talk when I have a beautiful woman on my arm—even American businessmen know there's a time and a place for everything. Besides," he said with maddening self-confidence, "I have my reputation to protect."

"And what about my reputation?" she asked, only half-seriously. "Won't it suffer from being here alone with you?"

"Indeed not! It will only make you more sought after in Cassar," he teased with an accompanying chuckle.

"Vanity, thy name is Karim El Hareembi," she softly taunted, and then laughed at the feigned hurt expression she could dimly see in the glow of a distant lamp. He could be lighthearted and amusing when he wanted, and that added even more depth to his overpowering attractiveness.

Karim's attention was arrested by the infectious quality of her laughter. She laughed often, he realized, and it was a very pleasant sound. At once it reminded him of the lack of such a sound in his own household. But then his attention wandered again...the full moonlight gave her blond hair a pale yellow sheen, and he found his self-control slipping, eroded by her loveliness. Her silhouette, framed by the beauty of the garden around them, was irresistible, and compelled by a longing he could neither deny nor understand, he reached forward and pulled her gently, purposefully, into his arms.

Surprise robbed Lindsay of speech, but she stiffened with passive resistance, and the fingers of her hands splayed out against his robe to push, ineffectually, against his chest. "What are you doing?" she whispered, the pulse at her throat and the blood in her veins beginning to pound with an excitement she'd never before experienced.

"Come, Lindsay," he softly chided. His hand reached up to comb the fringe from her forehead, then slid along the side of her cheek under her chin to tilt her face upward. "Don't try to tell me you've not been in a man's arms before?"

"Of course I have...m-many times," she stammered the exaggeration. *But no one made me feel faint, like you do, and I ... feel as if I could fly to the moon.* A confused mixture of feelings raced through her, and she fought desperately to enforce control over them-and over what was happening. But she couldn't think straight. She couldn't think at all, she admitted. Her senses were simmering with so many different sensations that were alien, because of her closeness to this particular man.

She watched his head dip toward her and knew she was going to be kissed and also that she was powerless to stop it. Her knees suddenly went weak, and she found her hands lifting to cling to his shoulders for support. "This is... madness..." she whispered.

"I agree, my lovely, but I've wanted to do this since I saw you on the staircase tonight and, madness or not, I cannot resist you."

In a blur she saw his approaching lips, and then all conscious thought fled as his mouth came down and covered hers. The touch of his lips sent electric tingles coursing through her, and a burst of pure heat began to coil low in her loins. His was a searching, sensitive kiss, a tender exploration of her mouth. But to her disappointment it ended far too soon.

When he drew back his head she opened her eyes, blinked and stared up at him, regretting that he had ended something they were both enjoying. When his hands dropped and encircled her waist to bring her closer to him, so close that she could feel his heartbeat hammering through the material of her gown and against her breasts, delicious waves of desire began to flick over her in a steadily increasing flow. And his eyes, black in the moonlight, were studying each of her features with an intensity that brought a warm flush to her cheeks even before he spoke.

"Sweet, desirable Lindsay... Are you aware of what you do to me? Do you know how long it's been since I've held a woman in my arms like this? Do you?" he asked, his tone softly seductive.

She heard the passion vibrating in his voice and couldn't answer; she could only shake her head, for she was overcome by her own response. Deep inside and low in the depth of her being a longing was setting her aflame for the first time in her life. And the need was so powerful it threatened her well-developed sense of self-preservation. But for the moment she didn't care. She wanted this dark, rugged sheikh of the desert to sweep away her inhibitions and make love to her. What he had aroused in her with one kiss made her tremble with desire for more.

He seemed sensitive to her mood and smiled as if he knew what she wanted. His mouth came down again to claim hers, this time with a passion that made them cling to each other. His tongue thrust deep into her sweet caverns seeking, plundering, commanding and getting a response that she couldn't deny him. Darting, ever-increasing waves of need washed over her body. Her fingers began to caress the thick column of his neck and twine into his mass of leonine hair. Their bodies fitted together as if they had been made expressly for each other, she noted with pleasure.

Indeed it was madness, she thought, but it was a divine, tantalizing madness that had come over both of them.

They remained entwined, lost in the wondrous embrace until the sound of footsteps approaching along the gravel path broke the spell. With a regretful sigh, Karim's arms dropped to his sides.

There was a distinctive, discreet masculine cough and then, "Karim?"

The owner of the voice came into view. It was Prince Zoltan, the emir's heir apparent, whom Lindsay had met at Shalima Palace and again earlier in the evening.

"Yes, Highness," Karim said.

"My father wishes to see you immediately. Some—" he paused and with a lift of one eyebrow added "—crisis." The young man spoke intensely, his interest in the affairs of the State of Cassar, which he would one day rule, patently obvious. "I believe the matter requires urgent attention, First Minister."

Karim turned to Lindsay, the memory of their kiss still in his caressing gaze. "Excuse me, but I must attend him."

"I will escort Miss Pentecost, er . . . Lindsay, back to the palace," Prince Zoltan offered.

Karim smiled at her once more before turning on his heel to return to the palace. She watched him stride away, unable to tear her gaze away from his magnificent, retreating figure. His kiss had knocked her for a loop and awakened a depth of sexuality she hadn't realized she possessed. And...but...shouldn't she have been angry with him for taking...advantage of her? The breath caught in her throat, and she paused mentally to wonder why she wasn't upset.

"My father's conferences usually last several hours," Prince Zoltan informed Lindsay. "I am sure Karim would want me to see you safely back to Shalima Palace. When you're ready to go, of course."

"I'm ready now, Your Highness," she told him. She needed to be alone, she knew. To think. To try to make sense out of what had happened between them tonight. The passion that had erupted—was it transitory? Would she, when she saw him again, feel nothing? Or would what happened between them create an avalanche of feelings she had no control over? Prince Zoltan's voice intruded into her thoughts.

"I have organized the sheikh's limousine to return you to Shalima Palace, Lindsay."

She murmured her thanks and, conscious of the curious gazes of many at the function, was personally escorted by the crown prince to the waiting vehicle.

Lindsay settled beneath the covers of the wide divan but sleep eluded her. She was still keyed up over the evening's events, but most of all it was Karim's embrace in the moonlight that caused the feeling of restlessness within her.

She had never before been kissed like that; nor had she ever responded with such abandon. The memory of her behavior made an arrow of heat course through her body. But had his kiss been merely an impulse of the moment? Was it just a man surrendering to a woman on his arm in a romantic setting? Should she read something deeper into his embrace?

With a groan she rolled onto her stomach, and before succumbing to tiredness she decided that she was not going to fall in love with the Sheikh of the Morasqs. No. Definitely...not!

Squeals of laughter made Lindsay glance up from the homework she was correcting at her desk in the schoolroom. The sound was infectious, and from her position she could hear the children splashing happily in the pool. Because of Hisham they weren't allowed to swim unsupervised so she knew that one of the staff, probably Tima, was with them.

She returned to her task, smiling with pleasure at Sonja's neatness as opposed to the hurried, untidy and often incorrect calculations of her twin. Darius had finally relinquished his resentment of her and now, apart from the odd bit of rebellion, they had settled into a friendship of sorts based on mutual respect. Academically he was the brightest of the four, though Sonja showed promise in the sciences.

She looked up from her work again to see an enormous splash wet the patio tiles and, curiosity triumphing, she rose from her seat and moved to the glass window to see what the imps were up to.

Her eyes widened when she saw the cause of the white wake—Karim—surfacing halfway up the pool. She hadn't realized that he'd joined the children in the water, and it was interesting to watch the way they swam to him and attacked him, each trying to wrestle him under the water, unsuccessfully, of course.

And Karim was like a big kid himself—a side of his nature she hadn't seen—splashing around and throwing Darius and Ali boisterously up in the air. But he was wonderfully gentle with Hisham, whose fear of the water was still very real.

She soon forgot her work and stood with her nose almost touching the glass, watching them skylark. It was a tender family scene and it reinforced an opinion she'd formed earlier. Karim became another person when he was with the children. The statesman, imperious and often aloof, used to handling weighty problems and advising the emir, was a loving, affectionate father. And poignantly it illustrated the difference in her own childhood memories. She could barely recall her father ever playing with her as Karim did with his children whenever he could.

Her gaze became riveted on him, and from the anonymity of indoors she took pleasure in studying the sheikh. If a man could be described as beautiful, Karim Omar El Hareembi was that in the purest sense of the word. His broad-shouldered torso was well muscled, though when he found the time to work out she couldn't imagine, and across his chest and narrowing down in a V to his purple trunks was a thick mass of curling, black hair.

Her heartbeat quickened, and she had to acknowledge the reason. Him. With every passing day her attraction to him was growing, and the strength of the excitement such feelings aroused was progressively causing her great concern. She didn't want to fall in love with such a man as Sheikh Karim. They were worlds apart in just about every imaginable way. His manner irritated her independent nature. They had differing views on almost everything of importance. Culturally they were poles apart . . . and yet there was something about him that fascinated her, and that she couldn't deny.

Sonja looked up, and seeing her at the window, waved. Karim also saw her and beckoned with an autocratic wave for her to join them. After a reluctant sigh, she did.

The heat on the terrace was intense. As she sat down she pulled off the light blouse covering her shoestring-strap sun-frock and immediately regretted it. The action made his dark eyes rake speculatively over her bare shoulders.

"It's too hot to sit and watch," he stated. "Come," he commanded, "join us in the pool."

Instantly Lindsay bristled at his dictatorial tone, and the warmth of her earlier feelings toward him rapidly cooled. The pool was inviting, sure, but what made him think she had to jump obediently to his every whim, request and order? And so, contrarily, she shook her head, murmuring as her chin tilted defiantly, "Another time, perhaps."

She watched a bushy eyebrow rise inquiringly and silently groaned as their eyes locked together. She now knew from experience how much Karim enjoyed the battle of wills that often took place between them, though she, personally, found them draining.

"You packed bathers, didn't you?" he casually asked.

"Somewhere..." she said offhandedly. "I'm not sure where though." That was a fib. She knew precisely which drawer she had thrown them into when she had unpacked.

"I'll help you find them, miss," Sonja offered. The young girl quickly climbed out of the pool and picked up a towel to dry herself.

"That's kind of you, Sonja," Karim put in, tongue in cheek. He found himself enjoying the brief play of annoyance that darkened the tutor's expressive face because he knew he had caused the reaction. Lindsay was, he already knew, an independent woman who resented being ordered about like a child. Yes, he mused to himself, he would have to remember that in future and try to be more subtle.

Drat the man, Lindsay thought crossly. He knew she wouldn't create a scene in front of the children. And oh, how he delighted in trying to manipulate her. He'd probably been doing it to people for years; it came to him as naturally as breathing did. But she didn't like it, and somehow she would show him she didn't.

"Yes, miss. Do join us," Ali pleaded from the pool's edge and then followed up with, "Remember, you promised to show us some novelty races. Like they do at St. Justinian's."

"Good." The sheikh's deep voice sounded his approval. "I'd like to see those novelty races myself."

Lindsay gave him a killing look and silently admitted defeat. It would be churlish to continue to refuse when the children were looking forward to her participation. But before she left she threw Karim a glance that clearly showed her disgust at his subtle manipulation. In the next instant she almost gasped with outrage when his eyes widened with triumph, as he silently acknowledged himself the victor in this particular clash of wills.

When Lindsay returned, towel in hand, she saw that Karim and Hisham were out of the water. Watching him towel his small son dry—he was so affectionate and gentle with him—her anger melted. And though it was courting trouble, she couldn't resist the urge to look at him. Her long, single glance confirmed what she already knew: the sheikh was a superb physical specimen.

It was just her luck, or rather the lack of it, that he should turn and catch her staring. He smiled a bold, composure-destroying smile, one which seemed to imply that he could read her thoughts and that he agreed with them. In turn his own gaze became active, thoroughly appraising her from head to toe and missing nothing of interest in between.

Her skin began to tingle, then to warm, her cheeks red-
dening under his bold scrutiny. But she dared not flinch or
show embarrassment. That was what he expected. Neither
should she cover herself, though her black one-piece suit
was quite modest by the current standards. *He's used to
looking at women in such a fashion,* she tried to convince
herself. *He's an Arab sheikh and considers himself master
of just about everything in his domain. Except me,* she
vowed. But as he approached her, her throat muscles
tightened nervously, and when he spoke she heard a huskiness in his voice that wasn't normally there.

"You look quite ravishing in that costume, Lindsay," he
said, his glance sliding meaningfully to the children. "It's
as well that we have four small chaperones, otherwise I
might reveal how much you tempt me," he whispered.

She murmured a shocked "Karim!" and then, suddenly
desperate for some distance between them, she dived for the
safety of the pool to cool the rush of heat spreading
through her body like wildfire. She wished he wouldn't say
things like that. Even if he was joking. They were quite in-
appropriate...and worse, thoroughly unnerving. She
wondered if he were joking. He'd spoken provocatively to
her before and when he did, her ability to stay calm and
cool quite deserted her.

She was not permitted to dwell on the interchange between herself and Karim, for Darius, Ali and Sonja soon
surrounded her, and she had to sharpen her wits to get into
the role of instructor. For a good half hour they frolicked
in the water together, Lindsay teaching them several novelty games at which Darius, in particular, excelled. But
when Mati came onto the patio bearing a tray of light refreshments the children abandoned Lindsay, clambering
out of the pool to wolf down the fruit and cheese platter
and the glasses of iced fruit juices.

Karim shook his head in despair at the absence of good manners, which made Lindsay laugh low in her throat. His thoughts said that clearly these mannerless cretins couldn't be of his blood.

Finally it was time to restore order, so Lindsay said, "Not so fast with the food, children. Anyone who gets indigestion from eating hastily will have to spend the rest of the day in his or her room." The threat worked, and they quickly settled down.

Mati served her and the sheikh with a separate tray of iced tea and small richly glazed pastries at another table. And Lindsay, mindful of Karim and his probing eyes, wrapped the large towel around herself, like a sari, to effectively disguise her curves.

But he didn't let her action pass without notice or comment. "You're too late, I'm afraid. I've already seen how delectable you are and committed you to memory."

She gave him a look of pure exasperation and hissed at him, "Will you stop saying such things, please? The children will hear."

But he was not in the least concerned. "So? I have nothing to hide."

That only made her groan and plead, "Karim, *min faDlak*." The look in her eyes was a plea she hoped he'd respond to. "You're making the situation impossible for me."

His gaze moved to the children. They had demolished the food and were heading noisily toward the playroom, but even so he leaned forward so only she could hear. "I do not understand you. Since the emir's dinner you've acted as if I had the plague. I . . . I . . . hoped our friendship might become—" he paused, his tone taking on an unusual huskiness "—more."

"Because you kissed me in the emir's garden?" The encounter had been in her thoughts constantly since its occurrence. "Don't give it another thought, Karim. I haven't." And she silently congratulated herself on how convincing the lie sounded.

He reached out and took hold of her arm to prevent her from moving away. "What does that mean?"

She stole a furtive glance at him from under her lashes and realized her remark had offended his Arab pride. She looked away again. "I...it's just that I understand that...that we...were affected by the mood, the moment! The perfume from the flowers in the garden, the moonlight, the entertainment. It all combined to make a...romantic interlude, that's all." He continued to stare at her and while everything she'd said was a pack of lies she brazened it out as best she could and put on the most serene expression she could manage.

"You were not annoyed, or offended?" he queried, his hold still on her arm.

"Of course not. I—" She swallowed the nervous lump lodged in her throat. "I've been kissed before, you know." But never, her pulses raced, by someone like you....

"Or affected by the touch of my lips on yours, the feel of my hands caressing your hair, the mingling of our body warmth?"

His verbal assault on her senses was so unexpected she couldn't think straight. She closed her eyes, hoping it would block the memories from her mind, but it didn't.

"Aaahh, emerald eyes," he whispered passionately. "I, on the other hand have been unable to think of anything else."

In a burst of enlightenment he knew it would take great patience on his part to win her trust. She was a beautiful, desirable woman but she was also stubborn, and he sensed that inside she nurtured a fear of, or possibly an aversion to men. Should he let her get used to their being friends first before anything else? Curbing his natural aggressiveness, his tendency to command affection rather than request it, would not be easy for him to do. It would take great self-control to achieve, he admitted, but, as his gaze rested on her again, he realized that the rewards could well be worth it.

"I confess that you confuse me, but if friendship is all you desire, Lindsay Pentecost, then so be it." *But just for the moment, my dear, just for the moment!*

Lindsay's gaze narrowed. She knew that was not what he'd intended to say. Something had made him change his mind. What? Her words, or her reaction? By now she understood the sheikh's character well enough to know that when he wanted to say something he usually had no difficulty in voicing his thoughts. And she also knew he was infinitely more clever than she was in dealing with people. That was why she was not comforted by his saying he'd be satisfied with friendship. That didn't sound like the sheikh at all. Still, she would have to accept it at face value—for the time being.

To mask her confusion she thanked him in a soft tone, "*Shukran*, Karim. I'm glad you understand."

"Oh, I did not say I understood, but if kismet decrees it, then it will be so."

And she had to be satisfied with that. She simply nodded and walked away, her spine stiff and straight, terribly aware of the feel of his eyes on her.

Couldn't he see how different they were? They were worlds apart! And her cool English common sense told her that if he couldn't or wouldn't see it, she could. She was not going to ruin her life by becoming involved with a totally unsuitable man.

As Lindsay left and he was alone, the ghost of Yasmin's face swam before his eyes once more and smiled as if she approved. Karim blinked and the vision disappeared but with it blossomed a sense of freedom, of peace, feelings he had not known for years. Was it now time to heal the wounds of the past? To start afresh?

He glanced at Lindsay's retreating back and had to acknowledge the sudden rapid beat of his heart. She intrigued him so much. More than any other woman. She was unpredictable and intelligent, and she had spirit as well as great charm. And, he confessed, he wanted to know her a good deal better than he did. But she was as wary as she was beautiful, and he would have to tread cautiously with Miss Lindsay Pentecost.

How to go about dismantling her reserve, her fears? Yes, that was a problem. He rose from the chair, his forehead puckering in a frown of concentration, and as he made his way to the office he began to plan.

Halfway there he changed direction and headed for his own quarters, deciding not to work tonight. He chuckled under his breath at the change in his normal routine. The emir thought he worked too hard, and usually, it was true. Since his wife's death he had welcomed the heavy work load to help mask the pain of his loss and the guilt. But now, since Lindsay had come to Shalima, he was discovering that there was more to life than just work. Yes, he smiled broadly, he hoped there would be much more.

Chapter Seven

"Lindsay."

She stopped in her tracks on the landing, arrested by Karim's imperious call. She waited patiently till he'd caught up. Then, looking sideways at his profile, she felt her pulses leap, so she hastily looked away and murmured quietly, "Good morning, Excellency."

"It's back to 'Excellency,' is it?" he asked with good humor.

Sighing, she corrected herself. "Karim." And then she started to move down the stairs.

"Lindsay, stop a minute. What's the rush?"

"The children. They're waiting for their first lesson."

"Selfish little devils, they can wait another minute or two," he said hard-heartedly about his own flesh and blood. "I want to know why you're avoiding me."

Halfway down the staircase she stopped to stare at him. "I...am not," she fibbed, "avoiding you. The children and I have been busy."

"So I've heard. Shareel reports that you've been clambering all over the town together."

"You don't approve of their going on field trips? They are intended as learning experiences, but if you disapprove I'll stop them."

"I'm not telling you to stop," he said in an exasperated tone. He didn't want to talk about her work; he wanted to talk about *them,* and she was being deliberately difficult. "It's . . . just that I've had so little time with them or you lately."

"You have been busy, you know," she threw in, suddenly desperate to have him believe it was as much his doing as hers. "Darius and Ali haven't been riding with you for a week."

And right on cue several youthful voices echoed from the bottom of the staircase. "Papa, Papa . . . Miss Lindsay."

Sensing her salvation, Lindsay skipped down the remaining stairs to greet them with, *"SabaaH 'alkhayr."*

"Good morning," they repeated in English to her.

"We came looking for you when you weren't in the schoolroom," Sonja said. "Ali thought you might be sick."

"I'm fine," she assured them. "Your father and I were talking. . . ."

"Yes," Karim said, joining them. "I was saying to Lindsay that we should all spend more time together. I've been busy lately, but the emir and the crown prince have gone to Baghdad for a few days so I can relax. I thought we might plan an outing together." He picked up Hisham, and Karim flashed a boyish grin at the children. "How about a trip to the Wadi of Sinjin?" he proposed and watched as they all—except Lindsay—nodded enthusiastically.

"Is there something special about a *wadi?*" she asked curiously.

"It's really a stream. The water comes down from the mountain snows, and because it is still spring it will be flowing well. We'll go tomorrow."

"Yes," the children chorused in unison.

"Have you forgotten, children," Lindsay put in, "to-morrow you're doing tests, important tests, too."

"Can't we do them after we come back from the *wadi*, miss?" Darius asked.

Lindsay was aware of several pairs of dark eyes studying her hopefully, and she was about to relent when the sheikh intervened.

"The tests are obviously important, children. We can easily go the day after tomorrow."

Lindsay's chin lifted mutinously. He was doing it again. Taking command—over her small domain, too. She had half a mind to disagree with him—to let them off the tests altogether—but at the last moment she changed her mind.

"And stay overnight, Uncle Karim?" Ali wanted to know.

"Overnight? It's that far away?" Lindsay queried.

"No, it's just a couple of hours' ride, but we start late in the afternoon and arrive at sunset, eat, and then camp out for the night. That's how we've done it in the past."

"Oh! It sounds like fun," Lindsay enthused, catching some of the children's excitement.

"But maybe Miss Lindsay doesn't ride," Darius remarked.

Karim's hand fell on his son's shoulder. "She does, Darius. It seems there aren't too many sports your tutor isn't proficient at."

"That's not true," she said, a warming flush coloring her cheeks.

"And what about Hisham, Papa? He can't ride that far," Sonja reminded her father.

"He can ride with me and with Miss Lindsay. I'm sure he won't mind that," the sheikh said, beaming a benevolent smile on his small son. "Then it's settled." He put Hisham down and gave them a collective push toward the classroom. "Now off you go and do good work for your teacher."

Watching Karim walk away, Lindsay shook her head in silent bewilderment. He had just manipulated her into spending hours, in fact an entire night, in his company and suddenly, for no good reason, she shivered. Karim El Hareembi was a force to be reckoned with. Warmth spread through her limbs as she recalled what he'd said by the pool days ago, and she was forced to wonder whether, if he really put all his energy into pursuing her, she would be able to resist him. A dominant, fascinating member of the opposite sex, he was unlike anyone she had ever met, but to fall in love with him would be the ultimate folly.

In almost military fashion Lindsay and the children assembled by their mounts, all of them watching as Karim fixed the wicker food basket to one side of Ali's horse. She saw that the children were almost bursting with excitement. Sonja's eyes in particular were shining with pleasure at being included, finally, and being able to ride her beloved pony, Shalimar.

Lindsay fiddled with the bridle of her own horse, checked the saddle girth and then asked Darius, "Would you double-check that I've done up all the bits and pieces correctly? It's been ages since I've ridden, and I might have forgotten something important."

Darius' shoulders squared, and he gave her a smile. "Of course. Papa says one can't be too careful about the details."

"And he's right . . ." she murmured quietly. She glanced up at Karim who now sat astride his favorite stallion with Hisham, and she thought how magnificent he looked. He was dressed for the desert in tan jodhpurs, calf-high boots, a white shirt and a white muslin *kaffiyeh* to protect his head from the sun. But the belted holster and gun at his waist were potent reminders that this part of the world was still untamed. Looking at him caused the pulse at her throat to quicken, and a knot of desire tightened her stomach muscles. Her hands felt clammy and she wiped them on her jeans, and all the misgivings that had kept her awake for most of the previous night resurfaced momentarily to dominate her thoughts.

"Mount up." Karim gave the order, and they all obeyed. "Darius, you and Ali take the lead, single file till we're through the old quarter, then go at whatever pace you like."

Darius responded with a military-type salute and "Yes, Papa."

He was being groomed to be a leader of men. Possibly the young boy wasn't even aware of it, Lindsay thought. In the next instant she found herself wondering whether his father had been groomed the same way. It would explain a lot if he had been.

Sonja followed Ali, then Lindsay, and Karim with Hisham brought up the rear. Lindsay could feel his gaze boring into her back, and self-conscious of it, she sat as straight as she could in the saddle.

The sheikh urged his horse alongside hers and casually asked, "How long has it been since you've ridden?"

"About a year or maybe a little longer," she answered after a moments deliberation.

"Then you'd better relax in the saddle a bit more or you'll be stiff and sore by the time we get to the *wadi*," he advised, then nudged his mount forward again and rode in tandem with Sonja.

The route they took out of town skirted much of the old quarter where the cobbled and packed dirt streets were narrow and crowded with various artisans and traders plying their wares. Many of them used the streets as open workshops. She visited this part of the city often, and its age and diversity still fascinated her. It was like stepping back a thousand years in time—so little had changed—and it made her grudgingly appreciate the thrill her father must have experienced when he had uncovered ancient works of art.

From Shareel she'd learned that the people called her *blanc infidèl* because of her fairness, and while she didn't consider herself vain, the nickname pleased her. It was better by far than "Nordic Iceberg" as she'd been dubbed in college, and which she now knew she wasn't. She liked to walk among the people, listen to their gossip and chat with them if they welcomed her, which they often did. She enjoyed bartering over a bag of nuts or a fragrance or an item of clothing, knowing the traders enjoyed the haggling too and were much more adept at it. She looked past the higgledy-piggledy apartments of dried mud bricks to where the city's skyline was slowly changing. In some ways it was a scaled-down version of the Cairo she remembered as a child, a quaint mix of antiquity and progress, and its very difference to Ontario and England struck a deep, responsive chord in her. Somehow—she had no idea why—she felt an affinity with Cassar, a belonging, which made little sense other than that perhaps she had some of her father's archaeologists blood in her after all.

She mopped her forehead and upper lip where beads of perspiration were forming. Karim, looking back and seeing her action, slowed his horse and smiled reassuringly.

"It will get cooler soon," he said and pointed to where the sun was close to setting behind the jagged mountain range. "By the time we reach the *wadi* you'll need a sweater. I hope you packed one."

"I did, as you instructed."

The sarcastic edge was not lost on him she noted with satisfaction. His eyes held hers for only an instant—although it felt much longer—and she saw something, an expression she had not seen before, which both thrilled and alarmed her. Lately he was not even bothering to hide the fact that he wanted more of her company. And his directness made her wonder if he had organized this outing to achieve some specific goal. If he had, he'd be disappointed, she promised herself. There were four small, noisy chaperons on this trip, and to keep him at arm's length all she had to do was keep one of them with her at all times. Yes. It sounded fine in theory, but whether it would work in practice was another matter.

"You look serious, Lindsay. A penny for your thoughts?"

"Uh-uh," she declined. "You wouldn't like them."

"Aaahhh," he murmured and immediately his interest was kindled. "I see. . . ." He knew she had been thinking about him. He did not consider himself a particularly vain man, but at times it rankled that this Englishwoman could remain cool toward him. Particularly when he was taking pains to be at his most charming. But was she as impervious to his attentions as she made out? Or was she simply more skillful than he'd realized at hiding her reactions?

It was his hope that during this excursion he would succeed in wearing down her defenses, her cool English reserve, and making her confess to the mutual attraction that continued to grow.

Hisham started to squirm in his father's arms and said, "I want to ride with Miss Linsy, Papa."

"Do you, you wriggling worm? Well, Miss Lindsay mightn't want you, you know," he teased and grinned wickedly.

She gave him a look that said as eloquently as words that she didn't approve of such teasing and held out her arms to the small boy. "I want you, Hisham, come here."

But as he transferred Hisham to her outstretched arms, Karim whispered softly, "Lucky boy," for which he received another dark look. "Sure you don't mind?" he asked again, as he settled his mount by reining in firmly.

"I'm sure." And, noting his mount's restlessness she added, "Why don't you and Sonja have a gallop? I'll catch up at my own pace." The track to the *wadi* was well used, and as such even such a novice as she could follow it.

"Very well," he agreed, giving her a knowing look that said he wasn't misled by such an unselfish motive. "Why do I get the feeling I'm being organized so you can keep me at a distance?"

"If you think that, you have an overactive imagination," she replied as innocently as she could. After watching him gallop away she gave her horse a nudge with her knees to get it going. She looked down at Hisham's mop of curly hair, marveling at how warm his small body felt and how pleasant it was to hold him close. He was a part of Karim, of his blood. Perhaps that was why she felt a special bond with him and the other children.

She scanned the desert ahead of her. Sand dunes and valleys of pink-gold sand were slowly turning amber, then a pale brown in the setting sun. She had not expected the desert to be so beautiful, and it was poignantly so, yet it was also terrifying. The vast emptiness was beyond anything she could have imagined, and she suddenly recalled stories from her childhood of travelers losing their way and disappearing forever. And just thinking of it spurred her to put the horse into a faster gear, a jog trot, which made Hisham laugh with glee.

"Faster, Miss Linsy...like the wind..." he encouraged.

Coming abreast of a small rise one could not even describe as a hill, Lindsay reined in and looked ahead. A quarter of a mile in the distance lay the most astonishing sight—the *wadi*. A clump of greenness where all else was pastel and pale. It was an incredible, beautiful sight, and as she pointed it out to the sleepy child dozing in her arms she saw two riders galloping toward them. Darius and Ali waved and shouted, and she flicked the reins to spur her mount on again.

The boys guided her and Hisham to where Karim had set up camp. Lindsay, still bemused by so much greenery, heard the faraway sounds of flutes and tambourines. She stared enquiringly at the boys, and they grinned back at her mischievously.

"There's a small caravan on the other side of the *wadi*," Darius told her. "Papa said we could visit after supper."

Karim took Hisham out of the saddle, but before setting him on the ground he boosted him high in the air. The action really woke the boy up. "Hisham," he groaned loudly. "You will soon weigh a ton, and I will be too old and weak to lift you."

Lindsay smiled at Hisham's squeals as well as his father's words. She had seen Karim in swimming trunks, and from his muscled torso she knew it would be many years before his strength faded.

"Off you go and wash your hands in the stream before we eat," he commanded. "I shall call you when supper is ready." He noted Darius and Ali's conspiratorial glance and issued a warning. "There will be no visiting the caravan till after supper. Mark me now."

Darius, Ali and Sonja wandered off, and he turned his attention to Lindsay, who still sat astride her horse. "Do you intend to sit there all night?" he asked, smiling up at her. How he wanted her. More than any other woman, he acknowledged. His lips ached to kiss away the doubts she had about him. Just as his hands itched to caress her until she, like him, became mindless with longing. But he curbed his natural desire and stood waiting for her answer.

"I am thinking of getting down," she assured him with a rueful smile. "It's just that my body doesn't want to move, for obvious reasons."

"I thought you'd end up being stiff," he said, but not unkindly.

Gritting her teeth, Lindsay made to dismount. In the next instant she found two strong hands at her waist helping her down. His touch set her nerve ends tingling and caused her mouth to go dry. Why did he have this shattering effect on her? Why?

"Terra firma again." His tone was bantering, light, as he turned her body slightly so that she faced him. His hands moved up her forearms to her shoulders, his fingers lacing into her flowing blond hair. "Alone at last, my elusive one," he murmured triumphantly and bent to brush her startled lips with his own.

"Please...don't," she begged, already feeling delicate flames spring to life inside her. But fighting the feeling was so difficult. She purposefully placed her hands against his chest, palms down, and was about to push him away when his hands rose to cover hers, making escape impossible.

"Why are you fighting this...what we feel here?" he breathed and moved their hands over his heart.

She looked up into his face and felt her resistance melting, disintegrating under the warmth of his dark, liquid eyes. "B-because..." she started to stammer. "I...m-must. It...can't work. It would be mad to think that you and I, that we..." She couldn't finish the sentence, but silently she added, *And I couldn't bear to be hurt by you.*

A dark eyebrow shot up imperiously. "Why not?"

"We're too different. We can't agree...we argue over so many things," she told him. Just as they were arguing now. She was a woman who had her feet firmly planted in the twentieth century while he, though being modern in some ways, was bound by birth and culture to the mysticism and traditions of the East. How could they possibly reach agreement on that alone?

He smiled confidently again and teased, "But making up makes the arguments almost enjoyable, Lindsay. So they say."

"Stop twisting what I mean, Karim," she said crossly. Couldn't he see he was proving her argument? She was horrified by her own weakness. It would be so easy to succumb to temptation and let their natural urges take over but where would that end? With her suffering a broken heart, most likely. And the probability of that happening suddenly strengthened her resolve.

"I—you're not being fair and you know it. I've not encouraged you to think I wanted such attention, and I'm no passive Arabian woman who'll let you do as you will," she added with spirit.

There was no disputing that remark, he thought wryly as he let out a long, heartfelt sigh. Still, neither was he one to give up easily. "Are you being completely honest with yourself, Lindsay? Remember in the emir's garden? Remember by the pool? And just now. Do you deny you wanted to return my kiss?'' he probed, his eyes challenging her for a truthful answer.

"I'm not denying that I—'' she tried to suppress the shiver ''—find you attractive, Karim. It's just that I'm trying to be sensible. That way no one will get hurt.'' Especially me. She saw something indefinable flicker in his eyes.

"How typically English,'' he said, frustration making his tone a biting one. "Good old sensible Lindsay. Tell me, will your common sense keep you warm on cold, wintry nights?'' Suddenly he wanted to shake some sense into her, to make her realize how foolish her fears were, but he suspected she would react angrily. So, swallowing what he'd planned to say, he conceded that this round was hers.

They were different, they did argue, but that was a part of their attraction to each other. Lindsay couldn't see that, either because she didn't want to or she was afraid to. And so, fearing he would be overcome by the desire to take her in his arms and kiss her into submission, he opted for an orderly retreat. He turned on his heel and stamped away from her.

Tima had prepared a feast for their supper, and all Sonja and Lindsay had to do was set it out, picnic-style, on a crisp white linen cloth. The children were ravenous after the long ride but, conscious of their father's watchful eye, their manners this time couldn't be faulted.

That the adults neither ate much nor spoke to each other went unnoticed by the children, their thoughts and chatter plainly centered on the caravan across the *wadi*—doubly so because Darius had earlier seen a soothsayer moving among the tents begging for food.

"May we go now, Papa?'' Sonja asked, jumping up as soon as she'd scraped her plate clean.

"When we have all finished and tidied up. I do not want you wandering off in four different directions. We will go together."

"We can all help clean things up," Lindsay said, "then we can go sooner."

"That's women's work," Ali answered and both he and Darius folded their arms in youthful defiance.

"In camps and caravans there is always a fair division of work between men and women," Karim told them, "and it will be the same here. Women have prepared the meal, so it is fair that the men help clean up." And so stating he began to stack the plates preparatory to rinsing them in the stream. The boys were so surprised to see a man as powerful as the sheikh doing menial work that their mouths gaped open. And to encourage them further, Karim added, "Those who cannot or will not help must stay behind and prepare the bedding for us when we return."

That got them moving, and it took little time before everything was tidy again. Karim put more logs on the fire so it wouldn't burn out, then he turned and said with an accompanying clap of his hands, "Shall we visit the caravaners or would you like to go to bed instead?"

"The caravan," they all shouted, and he waved them on ahead.

In single file they hopped across the stepping stones exposed on the *wadi*'s gently flowing stream to the other side where half a dozen tents, their material flapping in the evening breeze, were strung out in a semicircle. As they moved closer the sound of people talking and a plaintive tune being played on a flute rose above the quiet of the evening. A dozen or so camels, tethered to a feed line, were munching contentedly on dried grass, and around a communal fire women dressed in their traditional *abayas* were cooking the evening meal. They kept their eyes downcast as the strangers passed, but Lindsay didn't—she was as curious as the children about these desert nomads.

The men were gnarled, bearded, tough-looking tribesmen who, according to Karim, roamed the mountains and the desert plains bartering wares with the small groups of people who still populated what Lindsay had heard described as the most inhospitable region in the world.

Karim found the headman and went over. After the formal greetings and much salaaming, he sat down cross-legged on a handwoven mat to talk and exchange cigarettes. Two veiled women brought trays containing small glasses of a special herb tea sweetened with honey and rice cakes. Lindsay, seeing she was persona non grata in this male-dominated group, sought out the children.

They were clustered around a grizzled man dressed in ragged clothing. He was telling a story, a long-ago tale of an Arabic battle between two desert tribes. The children, agog at his clever weaving of a classic tale of conflict, made space for her to join the circle. The old man looked up, acknowledged her presence with an almost imperceptible widening of his crinkled-up eyes and then, ignoring her completely, continued the tale.

When it was finished and the applause had quietened, Sonja said to her in a respectful, hushed tone, "His name is Udan. He is a fakir of great renown. He wanders the Eyes of Allah mountains through all seasons telling his tales and reading the future."

"He will read our palms for half a *dirham* each," Ali said.

"That much!" said Lindsay, pretending it was an exorbitant amount.

"The headman's sons say Udan does it very well," Darius defended.

"Does what well?" Karim's deep voice questioned from behind.

"Reads palms, Papa."

"Perhaps." He looked at the aged, grizzled man who as yet had not seen him and said in a clear voice, "*In sha' allah*, old friend." Karim's outstretched hands were immediately clasped by Udan's wrinkled ones.

"Karim of the Morasqs," the old voice suddenly quavered. "Many seasons have passed since we sat on a mat together and talked."

"Too many, friend of my father. These—" he pointed to the children "—are my children, and this is their teacher, Miss Pentecost."

"They are fine, strong-looking children, Karim," Udan said. He held up his hands and made a blessing. "May Allah protect all of them."

"Will you read our palms, wise one?" Darius asked politely.

"Yes, young man."

And in turn he read the four children's palms. Hisham, notorious for being ticklish, tried not to giggle when the fakir's bony finger traced the lines on his small, pudgy hand.

"Now you, Papa." Sonja looked up at him, beseeching him to join in.

"My palm's been read before," Karim told them. Then he cast a sideways glance at Lindsay and said, "But if Miss Lindsay will have hers read, I will, too."

"But I don't . . ." She'd been going to say that she didn't believe in such things but Sonja's eager smile silenced her. What harm could it do? Still, with some trepidation—she was certain the old man's hands were none too clean—she let Udan take her hand. He stared into her eyes before looking down and studying the lines of her palm, then was silent for so long that she thought he had nodded off.

"I see strange things in this infidel's hand," he finally muttered. "Her spirit feels kinship with the sands of Cassar though her roots are from a faraway land."

Anyone could see that, Lindsay thought skeptically. The man's a fraud.

"She has known rejection from a blood tie for no just cause, and her heart has been made heavy because of it." He glanced meaningfully from her to Karim and went on. "The one to awaken you is close at hand, infidel, but I see danger...near the water...beware the seashore." Then he dropped her hand and made a salaam, an astonishing action as she was a woman and a foreigner to boot.

Karim frowned at Udan's words. *Danger, beware the seashore,* he had said. What did the old man mean? Was he in some obtuse way referring to Yasmin's untimely death? No, he thought not. The warning was aimed at Lindsay, and somehow he would have to put the seashore around Cassar off limits to her.

He made a small grimace in the dim light and pondered over how he would convince her to heed his request.

While Lindsay absorbed what Udan had said in his odd, rambling way, her thoughts were running at full speed. Maybe he had mystical powers after all. He had been right about rejection; her father had rejected her simply because she wasn't the son he'd wanted. And Udan had also sensed the feeling she had for this strange, barren country. A feeling of belonging here. And was he also right about her feelings for Karim? Was she being cowardly as the sheikh had implied in not freeing her heart? She was so confused.

"Now you, Papa," Darius urged.

With a sigh Karim listened to what the old man had to say.

"The strength of the Sheikh of the Morasqs is one of his greatest qualities and it will be tested many times in his life. For the path he has chosen is strewn with obstacles to be overcome, which in time he will. But his heart will also know great joy again...for the one to fill the void in his life has entered his domain...."

One didn't have to be clairvoyant to decipher Udan's quaint phrasing, Lindsay decided, but evidently the children, who were already wandering back to the caravan's communal fire to listen to music, hadn't grasped his meaning. Their youthful faces remained unenlightened, and she sighed with relief.

Karim's eyes caught Lindsay's and held them for a moment. Then they too walked back toward the caravan. He smiled, and strangely there was no need for words between them. Udan had foretold that which he desired to come to pass, and Karim was determined that it would.

Chapter Eight

Sleeping bags had been designed by a sadist, Lindsay concluded as she turned over, or at least tried to, without becoming more entangled in the padded folds. Finally she gave up trying to be comfortable or asleep and stared up at the sky. Millions upon millions of stars twinkled down on her.

She was changing, she had changed greatly since coming to Cassar. It was as if she had discovered a wondrous new self, awakening from dormancy. And she knew the reason behind it: Karim El Hareembi. Exposure to him had made her aware of wants and needs as a woman, feelings she had sublimated deep in her character for longer than she cared to remember. Aware of the futility of trying to fall asleep now that her thoughts were centered on him, Lindsay unzipped the sleeping bag, stood up and stretched muscles that had been uncomfortable for too long.

She heard water gurgling in the *wadi* as it passed over the stepping stones, and it seemed to call her. Donning her sweater, she made a quick check of the sleeping forms. With the light from a half moon to guide her, she walked to the stream. Sitting on the bank, knees bent and hands hooked around them, she contemplated the night and the incredible peacefulness of the desert.

After a while she heard the unmistakable swish-crunch sound of footsteps in the sand behind her and turned sharply. It was Karim, his long desert cape billowing around his shoulders. Even with his hair disheveled from sleep he looked magnificent. A slim-hipped noble giant with features as sharp as the desert hawk itself, a man proud of his heredity and his achievements.

She groaned inwardly as she queried her interpretation of him and deliberated, not for the first time, the reason he seemed attracted to her. Was it because the nature of his work left him little time to socialize, and at the palace she was always nearby, at his beck and call, should he so desire it?

If so, possibly she was destined to be no more than a passing attraction, and that thought made her heart as heavy as the cast iron tureens from which she had seen the women in the caravan camp ladling spicy lamb stew.

He squatted on his haunches beside her and asked softly, "Can't you sleep?"

"No," she answered curtly. If she could sleep would she be watching the water bubble and ripple across the stones as it cut its way through the valley? she thought somewhat sourly.

"It's the unfamiliar surroundings," he assured her. "When I was a young man my father took time off from his duties to the emir, and I from my studies, and we traveled the ancient frankincense trail with a few servants. At first I found it hard to sleep out of doors—I'd never done it before—so I sympathize with you." And so saying he settled himself comfortably on the sand beside her.

The silence of the desert was overwhelming, and for several minutes not a word was spoken. Lindsay's senses were so tuned to the man sitting in companionable quiet beside her that she dared not move or breathe for fear of somehow breaking the spell. A light breeze began to stir across the dunes, rustling the low spiky shrubs on the *wadi*'s bank, and involuntarily she shivered.

"You are cold." It was more a statement than a question and before she could answer he loosened the folds of his cape and spread it around her shoulders.

Though light, the cloth was pleasantly warm. From somewhere deep inside she found the presence of mind to utter a stilted, "*Shukran,* Karim. Ummm...it gets surprisingly cool at night, doesn't it?" But she knew that. She was talking for the sake of talking, using words to diffuse the implied intimacy of sharing the warmth of his cloak.

"Lindsay."

She heard the change in his tone, the sudden raspiness, the heavier breathing and the hint of him moving closer to her. Then he was twisting the upper half of her body around so that she was partly facing him. Her pulse rate rocketed, the muscles in her throat tightened and her mouth went dry as the desert itself. Teetering on the edge of anticipation, she waited. He was going to kiss her, and she knew equally well that if she had any sense she wouldn't let him. Let him! Did she have a choice in the matter? Karim was a forceful, demanding man—a man who took what he wanted without asking a by-your-leave.

"Ahhhh...my sweet angel, there is no escaping me now," he said and breathed her name with a pleasurable sigh.

His hands moved to cup her face, and she saw them tremble—they actually shook slightly—and in turn she was shaken by the knowledge that he could be so affected by her.

"Do you know the agony you're putting me through?" he asked huskily, his face moving closer till his lips were only a fraction or two from hers while his fingers feathered caressingly over her cheeks.

"Agony... why?" she asked, and astonished herself by adding, "Is my company so painful to the Sheikh of the Morasqs?"

His eyes lit with delight, and he whispered back, "You would dare to tease me?"

No. Never. Her heart was beating madly, and no words would come. She wasn't capable of teasing him, or thinking, only feeling.... Groaning low in his throat, he dropped his hands to her shoulders and pulled her roughly to him. He set his lips to hers, crushing them in a kiss so passionately demanding, so urgent and hungry, that she was swept instantly with him to the heights of desire. Her lips parted willingly to accommodate the sensual play of his tongue and to respond with a wantonness she couldn't control. He was setting her aflame with feelings she'd never experienced. She moved closer, slowly trailing her fingers up his forearms, over his shoulders, relishing the feel of muscles that tensed at her touch, until she found the curling ends of his hair and threaded her fingers through them. And all the while the sensible part of her brain was telling her to resist. But it was pointless. She was no longer strong enough to withstand the onslaught of Karim's—or her own—passion.

He moved a whisper away, his labored breath fanning her cheeks. Then with tormenting, light caresses his lips slid to the hollow of her throat while his knowing, tender hands

worked magic on her body, molding her to him. But it was
her lips that seemed to fascinate him, and soon his mouth
returned there. He kissed her again and again, ravishing
their softness with a consuming ardor, using his lips as
masterful, all-conquering weapons as he pressed her body
back and down into the desert sand.

She felt his hand slip beneath her sweater, then snake
upward to find and cover the soft mound of one breast. She
barely managed to stifle a gasp as a shiver of pure pleasure
ran through her. She couldn't, *didn't,* want him to stop. She
wanted more. His knowing caresses had awakened a passion she had only dreamed she might possess, and as sensation on top of sensation rioted through her she gave up
any pretense of passivity.

But, a small sane part of her mind wondered, where were
the fine resolutions she'd once made about keeping him at
a distance? *Gone* . . . for he had found the key and opened
a floodgate of emotions she could no longer deny. Logic
was now beyond her, and she knew that she would go where
her heart led her and suffer the consequences later.

A shock wave of disappointment rushed through her
when, all of a sudden he sighed and moved away. He sat up
and ran a hand through the hair she had helped to muss up.

Lindsay's feeling of loss was so acute that words sprang
from her lips before she was consciously aware of saying
them. "W-what's the matter? Did I do something . . .
wrong?" She had thought they had been doing everything
wonderfully right.

He looked at her, gave her a fleeting smile and touched
her cheek gently. "No, my angel, it is not you. I fear that
timing is against us. Can you not hear the sound of the
caravaners? Already their camp is stirring to life, eager to
start the day because of the heat. And soon the children will
wake and want breakfast before we leave for home." He

sprang to his feet and reached down to pull her up, brushing the odd twig or two from her hair and the sand from the back of her sweater. "Alas, we will have to continue—" his black gaze swept over her with barely controlled yearning "—another time. When things are right for us to travel the road to paradise, my dear one, I want it to be perfect for us both—not a hurried coupling that is finished before it's begun."

She colored rosily in the predawn glow at his frankness, but while the veins in her body still pumped from needs unfulfilled, already sanity was beginning to prevail. He could have possessed her here on the sand, and she'd have let him. More than let, she would have welcomed his fierce passion and responded equally with her own, inexperienced as she might be.

"Come, we must return," he said, and with his arm threaded possessively about her waist they retraced their steps to their camp to be greeted by a sleepy-eyed Hisham awake and hungry.

Lindsay sat in the classroom quite oblivious to the voices of the children prattling noisily around her, her mind and emotions concentrating on the faint but unmistakable deep voice approaching. It was Karim of course, and suddenly her pulses began throbbing at a faster pace and with an excitement she had not imagined possible.

The man had ruled supreme over her mind and body since the night at the Wadi of Sinjin, and she was becoming quite paranoid about anyone, but especially him, discovering her feelings. She had thought long and hard on her unrestrained response to him that night—and of everything connected with him—and she finally concluded that only love would cause such a gigantic swing in her emotional state. Normally she was a calm, stable person who liked order and peace in her life, but Karim had completely disrupted that.

At first she had tried to convince herself it was infatuation; after all, she had never met anyone as magnetic before. But deep inside she knew it was more than a physical response. So much more. And then she had wondered what she should do about it. How should she react? Should she succumb to this glorious, all-consuming feeling, or fight it with what was left of her sanity?

Undoubtedly Karim would press for the former; she had noticed his steamy, searching stares on her for many days. But, in the long run, what good would come of it? A brief, torrid affair perhaps. He probably considered her no more than a passing fancy, someone to be enjoyed and then forgotten, like yesterday's news. And that she couldn't endure.

With difficulty she brought her concentration back to the matter at hand—teaching. "All right, children, finish up now and tidy your desks. The sheikh is home, and remember, he promised you a ride down by the old salt-mine site today." Lindsay was pleased that since the trip to the *wadi*, Sonja was included in such outings.

"Will you come with us, Miss Lindsay?" Sonja asked.

"Not today. I've had some clothes made to order, and I have to pick them up at the souk."

"Me come, too?" begged Hisham.

"Not today, dear. I'm going to be out way past your bedtime." And when his features looked crestfallen she boosted him up to her hip and gave him a quick hug. "But I'll bring you back something special," she added, for which she received an enthusiastic, sloppy kiss.

The classroom door opened then, and Karim witnessed Hisham's embrace. He smiled as he noted Lindsay bravely coping with his youngest's exuberant show of affection.

Striding toward them he asked, "Got any hugs for me, Hisham?" and took the solidly built youngster from her. His dark gaze locked with her green eyes and he whispered, "Aahhh...my sweet, desirable Lindsay. Tell me what I must do to get into your arms as easily as my son does?"

Somehow she controlled the fiery blush and, shrugging off her embarrassment as best she could, moved away as soon as he'd relieved her of Hisham. "If you were five years old, no trouble at all," she said with a lightness she did not feel.

The curve of his mouth thinned to a wry grin and he said with a sigh, "If I were his age, being in your arms would have an entirely different meaning."

In spite of herself she laughed. Karim's humor was one of the things she found particularly endearing, doubly so because with his dark, hawkish looks and diplomatic demeanor it was so unexpected.

"You scamps ready for a ride?" he addressed the other three children and then pretended to be deafened when they all shouted that they were. "Well, go and change. I want you at the stables in ten minutes."

Hisham, wriggling to be free, was set on the floor and followed the others out at a dead run, his small legs working flat out to catch up.

Karim closed the door and leaned against it, his eyes glittering with distinctive masculine mischief. "Alone at last," he murmured huskily, but as he tried to take her in his arms she adroitly side-stepped him and retreated behind the desk. He did not follow but stood studying her, his expression one of frustration. Finally, when he did speak, his tone was reproachful. "Lindsay...darling..."

She shivered, as much at his intimate tone as at his term of endearment. She held up a hand before he could con-

inue. "No, Karim, this is . . . us . . ." Oh, she was making a
ness of what she wanted to say. "It must...stop. Can't you
ee how impossible it is?"

"It is not impossible," he said confidently. "In fact, it
s imminently possible and in my opinion most—" he
aused, then went on with a dramatic lift of his eyebrow
"—desirable. Your fears are groundless, believe me, Lind-
ay." He moved closer to the desk, ignoring her continu-
ng retreat to the blackboard wall, and stated, "I am not
ormally a patient man—we of the desert never have been.
But I am trying to be patient with you because I know you
re unsure of yourself, of your feelings. But be clear on one
oint, my sweet, elusive angel, I mean to have you." And
o emphasize the point he reached forward and took pos-
ession of her hands while his dark eyes captured hers and
ared her to look elsewhere.

Anger, born partly from sexual tension and partly from
er well developed independent streak, mushroomed in-
ide Lindsay. "Do you, now? Don't I have a say in the
matter? Or are my wishes immaterial to the Sheikh of the
Morasqs?" she asked, her tone deliberately sarcastic.

"You think I would force you to do something you didn't
vant to do?" he softly queried. As if he could! She was no
asy-to-control, malleable woman. He saw the light of
attle glisten in her eyes, making her even more vivacious,
nd it made him want her all the more.

"You are a very powerful man—you said so yourself.
Powerful, determined men are capable of many things
thers are not," she said, fencing with him while desper-
tely wishing she could make a quick exit. Unluckily for her
is height and breadth blocked her only line of escape, and
hat made anger her only means of defense against the deep
eelings threatening to engulf her.

"I think you do not have a very high opinion of me, Lindsay," he said, sounding genuinely hurt. "I had hoped that, in time—"

"You'd undermine my resistance," she interrupted, "and I'd succumb to your obvious charms. Is that what you hoped, Karim?"

"I wouldn't have put it quite like that, but..." He left the rest unsaid and accompanied by an aggravatingly confident half grin, released her hands and thrust his own deep into his trouser pockets.

The man was impossible, she decided. Arrogant and overconfident in the extreme. He thought himself irresistible to women. The maddening thing was that to her, he was. But she wasn't idiotic enough to let him see that she thought so. "You're very sure of yourself, aren't you?" she argued, the anger fed by his presumption bubbling inside her again. "What makes you think I'll jump into your arms whenever you have an odd free moment to amuse yourself?" In truth, though, she had a good idea why he thought she would; she had done so too many times already.

Karim could feel his own temper rising and recognized the sense of confusion within him. Why was she reacting so angrily to what he had said? It was true, and she knew it. But in an attempt to placate her he pointed out huskily, "You belong with me. Udan told us so at the *wadi*. And fighting it will only bring us anguish when..." His restless hands reached for her again and drew her unresisting body against his. "All I want to do is bring us joy."

The effect of his words and touch was mesmeric. She tried to maintain her anger but couldn't, and when his lips caught hers she sighed and surrendered to the moment. Being in his strong, gentle arms was heavenly, and the per-

suasive ardor of his kiss transported her to a place where
feelings reigned supreme over any other consideration.

Karim was all any woman, particularly this woman,
could want. So why did she continue to put obstacles in
their path? She sighed and silently confessed that for days,
since their outing to the *wadi,* she had been fighting a losing battle against an overpowering force that was dominating her waking hours and her dreams. She gave in and
admitted for the first time that she loved him and wanted
him with a totality that frightened her, and the drumbeat
of her heart and her heightened senses attested to the fact.

Yet a part of her refused to believe it could ever be anything more than a brief, fairy-tale romance—like the many
stories she had read as a child. There were too many things
keeping them apart to allow for the happy ending. *They*
were too different and eventually wouldn't the differences,
the things that had always separated East from West, tear
them apart? Besides, she tried to rationalize, in the time he
had been pursuing her he had never hinted at having deep
feelings for her. His need was all physical, and because she
cared so much desire wasn't enough.

"My dear Lindsay," he murmured, his tone hoarse as he
rained short, passionate kisses on her face, her cheeks, the
nape of her slender throat and all the way down to the bare
shoulder of her sun-frock. "I need you so much...."

Minutes passed while they stood embracing until Karim
finally gulped in a deep breath. He stepped away from her
and once more rammed his hands into his trouser pockets.
His head fell to one side, and he regarded her silently for a
moment before saying in a tone full of emotion, "Perhaps
I should...whisk you off into the desert as my grandfather did my French grandmother. And make love to you
there till you acknowledge your feelings...."

She knew he was capable of carrying out such a threa and wisely refrained from comment. But the tension be tween them was escalating and, worse, she couldn't break away from that passionate gaze of his. It said much more than words to her. He wanted her to surrender completely to his will, but if she did she feared she would be forever lost and at his mercy.

For several enthralling seconds she imagined the plea sure of Karim making love to her on a bed of cushions in a bedouin tent, and she knew he would take her to the gate of paradise as he had promised. But what would happen to her afterwards, if his passion for her didn't last? What if she was, as she truly feared, a passing fancy to him?

"That's not . . . going to happen," she said with all the assurance she could muster. And she prayed that he would not challenge her. For if he did she lacked the willpower to push him away.

Karim's gaze narrowed on her, and suddenly all his pen up frustration exploded in an accusation. "So, you are a coward after all."

Goaded by his cutting tone she queried him. "What do you mean?"

"You are afraid of your feelings, Lindsay. Of what make you feel. You are afraid to let go and become a real woman."

He knew her too well, she realized, but even so, pride forced out the lie. "I am not." Cut to the heart, she tilted her chin upward and said coolly to him, "There must be many women in Cassar who would jump at the chance to . . . have your . . . attentions."

"Indeed there are," he said assuredly, while thinking that, unfortunately for him, she was the woman he wanted "Several, in fact, who are not afraid of their emotions, who know how to please a man," he added, hoping to raise a spark of jealousy in her. And in a restless spurt he began to pace the schoolroom floor.

"Well, go to one of them and leave me alone!" she shouted, her temper finally getting the better of her. Then suddenly she saw her escape route and, knowing she was on the brink of tears, rushed for the schoolroom door, the echo of his words taunting her.

"Perhaps I will." Karim's eyes widened in disbelief as he realized she was walking out on him—again—and he roared angrily, "Lindsay, come back." But she had already made it to the outside corridor.

His bellow halted her retreat, but only momentarily. She half turned back to him and threw over her shoulder, "Go to hell," then bolted toward her quarters, half-expecting him to follow and waylay her. To her relief, as the tears streamed down her cheeks, he didn't.

Wretched woman! In sheer frustration his hands balled into fists at his sides as he stood alone in the empty schoolroom, contemplating the scene. Why did he bother with her? he asked himself. She thwarted him at every turn, she was disrespectful, she would not surrender to 'is will. And her temper! God, she was magnificent when she was out of control. How he ached to have her that way in his arms. His jaw drew into a stubborn line, and he refused to admit defeat. He would have her. It was kismet, whether she liked it or not.

Alone in her quarters Lindsay made herself a light snack in the small kitchen. She then plonked herself down and turned on the VCR to watch the video she had borrowed from Karim's private library. It was supposed to be a comedy, but ten minutes into the movie she still hadn't found anything amusing. Maybe it was more her lousy mood than the film.

She jerked out of her mental lethargy on hearing a dis
creet tap at the door, and to her secret delight it was Karim.
She hadn't seen him for two days; he'd been off on a special
assignment for the emir. Just the sight of him looking par
ticularly handsome in an off-white three-piece business sui
aroused the hunger inside her, the love she couldn't deny
but to which she wouldn't surrender.

"Hello, Lindsay. May I come in for a minute?" he asked

"Hi, yes, of course. Come in. Would you care for a cof
fee or tea, or something to eat? Did the trip go well? Wa
the emir pleased with the result?" She babbled on, asking
one question after another, knowing how foolish her ner
vousness made her sound but unable to stop herself.

He merely grinned and answered, "No, yes, yes in tha
order," to her questions.

She blinked owlishly at his answers, at first not under
standing, then when she did she gave a low, nervous laugh
*Will you get a hold of yourself? He'll think you're a raving
idiot.* She strove to appear casual. "Please, won't you si
down?" She felt rather uncomfortable having him in her
quarters—he had never been farther than the doorway be
fore—and with his immense physical presence he seemed to
dominate the room.

"Thank you. I can't stay long, though nothing would
please me more."

"More work for the emir?" the tart question popped out
of her mouth before she could stop it.

"No. Darius and I are going to the horse traders auction
at the animal souk. He hasn't attended one before, and
promised he could come with me," he said, ignoring her
sly, verbal shot. Her show of temper pleased him, and he
interpreted it as a sign that she had missed him. Good
Then he remembered why he was there. "I wanted to ask
for your company tomorrow."

"Tomorrow, why Karim?"

"I'm going down the coast to inspect progress on a de-alination plant being built there. I thought you might enjoy the trip."

"Tomorrow is Wednesday, and it's a normal school day, isn't it?"

"It is, but I hoped you might—how do they say it in your country—" he appeared to think for a moment "—play truant for the day."

"Oh." His invitation, totally unexpected, threw her into confusion. "A-and the children . . . they can come, too?"

"They cannot," he said firmly. "A building site is no place for four inquisitive children. I've organized for Shareel to give them an outing on my yacht. They are going to the Island of Jabal, off the coast for the day."

"Oh," she said again and was then silent.

"You are not concerned about being with me, are you, Lindsay?" he asked frankly, having noticed her indecisiveness.

Yes, she confessed to herself, troubled by her mixed feelings. A large part of her was thrilled that they could spend time together while another warred with that emotion, telling her that it would be an unwise decision. Though his peremptory method of organizing things without asking her first should have annoyed her, in this particular instance it didn't.

"You have nothing to fear from me, you know," he said quietly.

"I know." Didn't he realize she was concerned for herself? He had such power over her, and if only he knew the extent of his domination she would be done for. "I'd love to come," she said, knowing that if she declined he would assume she was afraid. With a rush of independence, she knew she couldn't allow him that victory.

"Wonderful! I think you'll enjoy it. You've seen the desert and wandered all over the city streets with that camera of yours till you knew the place as well as I do. Now you will see our small coastline. Some people say it's harsh in the extreme but I prefer to call it rugged, and in some spots it's quite spectacular.

"Is the site far from Cassar?"

"A two-hour drive. We'll try to beat the heat by leaving early—about 7:00 a.m. You can meet me in the courtyard about that time." Reluctantly he moved toward the door saying, "I must go and change before I meet Darius. He's already impatient to get to the sale. I suspect he hopes I'll purchase another horse for him because Midnight is getting too old for him to ride. He needs a younger, stronger horse with spirit."

"Of course." She understood. As far as she was concerned it was one of Karim's strong points that, whenever he had a spare moment—and they seemed increasingly few—he spent that time with his children and Ali, who he treated as though he were his own son. It made the disparity between Karim and her own father more marked than ever. Why couldn't Harry Pentecost have been more like Karim? The sheikh was openly affectionate with his children, not cold and disapproving as her father had been to her. Her mother, Valerie, had tried hard to make up for her husband's disinterest, but even now the memory of his indifference hurt.

Karim opened the door wide and stepped out into the corridor. "Till tomorrow. Wear something cool and sensible shoes. And—" his sweeping glance was almost a caress "—sweet dreams, Lindsay."

He moved off with confident strides toward his apartments, which were on the next floor. And that was just as well, he decided, knowing that if his rooms had been closer,

he urge to knock on her door on one of the interminably
ong, restless nights and make love to her might have over-
powered him.

Karim didn't like to be kept waiting, so Lindsay made
ure she was ready on time. As they drove through the city,
reading south, the tall, slender minarets echoed with the
mam's early morning call to the faithful to prayer.

"You're quiet this morning," he commented from his
position beside her in the back of the chauffeured limou-
ine. "Are they thoughts you can share with me?"

The deep timbre of his voice started a flow of warmth
within her, reminding her of how conscious she was of
him—and their shoulders were almost touching. But nat-
rally she couldn't tell him that. "Actually, I'm only half-
wake. I'm not used to rising quite so early."

"Are you sure that's all?" he pressed.

"Yes." She confirmed it with a half-stifled yawn.

"I'm sorry, but the early start was necessary because of
he weather." He took the opportunity to pat her hand, his
ingers lingering longer than necessary, enjoying the touch
f her skin. He was further tempted to pick up her hand
nd bring it to his lips, but he exerted enough self-control
nd finally withdrew his touch. She continued to be skit-
ish in his company, like a high-spirited filly. Was it be-
ause of their attraction to each other? he wondered. He
as, he confessed to himself, unable to keep her out of his
houghts for long these days. In fact his work output was
windling because of his preoccupation with the lovely
oman beside him, so much so that even the emir had
oted his lapses and, wily old devil that he was, guessed the
eason and been amused by it. In an effort to channel his
houghts into a different area, he began to tell her about the
roject they were going to inspect.

"You might like to know a few facts about the desali‑
nation plant, Lindsay. It's a four-year project and is half
completed. We sank many exploratory bores hoping to find
water as we had in the underground lake below the city, but
we found nothing, and finally it was decided to build a de‑
salination plant. It will pump sea water in, desalinate it, and
them pump it through underground canals to arable land
close to the site."

"It sounds an expensive and ambitious project," she
said, pleased to concentrate on something other than the
devastatingly attractive man next to her.

"The expense will be worth it in the long run. We have
students overseas studying farming and agriculture, and
when this plant is fully operational we will begin construc‑
tion of another in the north."

"It certainly shows forethought on the part of the emir."

She had noticed a lot of planning for the future in the
emir's tiny state. Hospitals and modern schools, new
housing—especially in the old quarter and the continuing
emergence of small factories no doubt subsidized by the
state.

They spent the remaining time discussing the many
projects Karim was involved in. He broke off during a de‑
scription of a planned cannery to say, "We are here," and
pointed to a vast building site that was like a Meccano set.
Tall buildings, some only half-completed, gigantic storage
tanks and bulldozers, cranes and graders.

"Because of the heat the laborers work broken shifts,"
Karim told her, "from 5.30 a.m. to 10.30 a.m., then they
break till five and work till sunset. Now that we're coming
into summer, all work stops for eleven weeks. They finish
this week, and that's why we're inspecting progress to‑
day."

"We?" she queried with an upraised eyebrow, then heard a whirring sound. A helicopter came into view and descended rapidly toward a marked-out helipad.

"The emir and Prince Zoltan," he told her as he motioned her into the closest demountable building to escape the rising cloud of dust.

From the window of the building, which was some kind of office, they watched till the dust had settled before venturing out to greet the royal party. The emir smiled as he recognized Lindsay, and her brief respectful salaam made his smile even broader.

"Lindsay, my dear, what a pleasant surprise," he said, then favored Karim with a reproachful glance. "You made no mention that your charming tutor would be accompanying you today."

"It was a last-minute decision, Highness," the sheikh said, clearing his throat with embarrassment.

"And one I am personally delighted with," Emir Abdullah said with a touch of old-world gallantry.

Two men in shorts and sweat-soaked shirts had driven modified golf carts with canvas roofs up to the visitors, and the emir took Lindsay by the arm and directed her to the first cart. "Come, we will inspect the site together before this heat dehydrates all of us." When they were both seated comfortably the emir tapped the driver imperiously on the shoulder and said, "Come on man, let's get to it."

During their thirty-minute tour of the site, the driver, who was in fact the supervising architect, an Egyptian, gave a steady commentary on the site's progress and some of the problems they'd had. But his words carried confidence, which was not lost on the wily emir, who could see, as could everyone else, that the project was progressing to schedule and to everyone's satisfaction.

132   THE SHEIKH

"Jayyid," the emir murmured, then turned to Lindsay and asked her opinion. "What do you think of this, it is a good idea, yes?"

"Yes, Your Highness, a very worthwhile project," she said politely and sincerely. "Karim explained much of its need on the drive here."

"Ahhh...and did he tell you that he devised and planned it all?"

"No."

"Humph," Cassar's ruler grumbled, "he wouldn't. The fellow's too modest. But let me tell you, young lady, he is behind a good deal of the recent improvements being implemented in our country. He and Prince Zoltan have a twenty-year plan, and between them they hope to make Cassar a twenty-first century Utopia. But I worry about him."

"Prince Zoltan, Highness?"

"No, Karim. The man works too hard," he confided. "He's become a workaholic lately—since poor Yasmin's death. We all know he's used the work as a means of coping with his grief, but he should learn to relax more."

"He is devoted to you and Cassar, Highness," she said somewhat defensively.

"I know that, but he should marry again," the emir muttered. "A man needs a wife to give him comfort—and children." He gave her a sly, sidelong glance. "Don't you agree, my dear?"

She shrugged her shoulders and managed to murmur casually, "Not being male or old-fashioned, Your Highness, I probably don't see things that way. Perhaps the sheikh is happy with his present life. Perhaps he doesn't feel the need to marry again. And he is busy. Anyone...who married him would have to be very understanding...and self-sufficient."

"Naturally," he said with an odd inflection in his voice. "Is it not a wife's duty to be so, Lindsay?"

"Maybe a Muslim wife, but in England? I'm not so sure. We tend to consider we have needs, too."

Her answer made him chuckle. "Well said, Lindsay. You are as direct as Karim said you were. Still, I think it is high time he freed himself of his devotion to my poor Yasmin and got on with the business of living. When he returns from his next trip we will discuss the matter of a new wife for him," he added blandly. "No doubt there will be many suitable candidates."

"No doubt," she repeated through dry lips, her thoughts in turmoil. The probability of the emir's arranging a marriage for the man she was in love with—knowing she would not be one of the candidates—plus the surprising news that Karim was going away again had thrown her into a real tizz.

"Uumm...Your Highness, this proposed trip of the sheikh's. I don't..."

"He goes away at this time of the year every year, my dear. Partly to escape the summer's heat. Hasn't he mentioned it yet?" he threw in casually. "The children go to the French Riviera, and he goes around the world on my behalf. I hate traveling, my dear. And this year, Prince Zoltan, now that he has finished studying at the University of Baghdad, will be accompanying him."

Lindsay digested this information with growing anger and hurt, seeing it as yet another indication of the sheikh's high-handedness. She didn't expect to be privy to all Karim's thoughts, but she did think he would have the good manners to tell her things that concerned her and her small charges. By the time she and the emir returned to their starting point she was quietly fuming. And when Karim came up to ask what she thought of the project it was all she could do to stop from snapping at him.

"Very impressive," she said briefly to him. When Prince Zoltan made some comment to her, she half turned away from Karim, not caring if any of these autocratic, dominating males were shocked by her show of disrespect for the First Minister of Cassar.

Karim recognized her mood and frowned. His gaze flashed from her to the emir, who was watching the play between them with interest, and the furrows on Karim's forehead deepened. Abdullah had said something to upset her—he knew from the mischievous expression on his ruler's face. But what? he wondered. And how would he get it out of her?

As the siren screamed the end of the morning shift, the visiting party was deferentially ushered into one of the air-conditioned demountables—a huge dining area—and a sumptuous, lengthy morning tea was offered them. Lindsay was the only woman present, and to say that she felt odd about that was understating it somewhat. She toughed it out and made certain she kept her distance from Karim, whose intermittent enquiring gaze she found disquieting and annoying.

Finally the social aspect of the royal party's inspection came to an end, and they exited into the daylight. The still desert heat hit them like a furnace blast, and consequently farewells were brief, as no one wanted to prolong the discomfort.

Karim's chauffeur came up to him, salaamed respectfully and begged a private word with him. A moment later the sheikh nodded in assent and then went and spoke briefly to the emir.

Lindsay stood waiting in the shade near the limousine, her clothes clinging to her body as she perspired profusely. She estimated the desert's power over mere mortals and decided that in this heat one could dehydrate in a couple of hours. Karim walked toward her and, safe in the anonymity afforded by her sunglasses, she studied his long, proud strides and grudgingly admitted that he was certainly something, this man of the desert. Love for him welled up inside her, paralyzing her anger and all movement for several seconds.

He opened the front passenger door and said, "Get in, Lindsay. The motor's running, and it's much more pleasant inside than out." He waited until she was seated and then advised, "The chauffeur's not well, so I'm sending him back to Cassar in the helicopter with the emir's party."

"You're going to drive?"

"Of course," he replied, then looked at her with extreme tolerance. "One of us has to unless I second one of the workers. But perhaps you'd care to don Faisal's hat and be my chauffeur? A much prettier one you'd make, too."

"No, thank you. One hat at a time—my teacher's cap—is enough for me," she said in a cool tone.

It took Lindsay ten minutes to work out that Karim wasn't driving toward Cassar, and she immediately tackled him. "This isn't the way to the city. Don't tell me there's another project to inspect?" Please say no, not in this heat anyway. He might be used to the Arabian summer, but she would definitely expire from it.

"No. Like you, I'm playing truant for the rest of the day. You recall I said we had some spectacular coastline—well, a little farther down the road, near a small fishing village, you'll see some of it. There's a special cove there. I thought we might have a picnic lunch—I had Tima pack one in ice early this morning."

Lindsay didn't say anything—for once she was really speechless. A picnic on a hot summer day? The temperature was over 110 in the shade! Was he mad? But she wasn't going to be put off any longer, and especially not by the promised lure of a picnic. "Good. On the way you can tell me all about this planned trip the children and I are taking at the end of the week." She paused for effect. "The one I know nothing about."

"Really?" He was genuinely surprised and pleased finally to learn the reason for her ire. "I thought Shareel had mentioned it to you. It's an annual event at Shalima. In the middle of summer the heat is rather fierce, and I take a six-week business trip around the world, checking on Cassar's investments...."

"I know that," she said impatiently, "the emir told me."

"Yes. Well, because I'm away, the children go to our villa on the Riviera. It has its own private beach with a small yacht anchored in the bay. The children love the place, the staff spoils them rotten and—"

"What about their lessons?"

"Oh, that's a very low priority. It's their seasonal holiday."

"And I'm expected to accompany them, I presume?"

"Other tutors have in the past. You could regard it as a holiday yourself. There's plenty of staff at the villa to watch the little ones, and Ali's mother, Monna, has been in residence for a month preparing everything. You'll like her, she's easy to get along with."

Even though she tends to forget that she has a son who needs her, Lindsay thought archly. His explanation had cooled her ire considerably, but the fact that it had been kept a family secret rankled. And as usual, Karim controlled everything. Maybe...just maybe she'd tell him she'd make other plans, just for the hell of it. But where could she go? She hadn't saved enough for a trip back home, or anywhere else that interested her. Besides, she would miss the children. She had become fond of all of them and they—

ves, even Darius—returned that affection. No, she'd accompany them to the Riviera.

And then it hit her—like a thunderbolt. She wouldn't see Karim for six long weeks. Oh, God, she had withdrawal symptoms when she didn't see him for a couple of days! Her mind went off in a kind of downward spiral just thinking about it. Oh, why did she have to care so much for him? The answer was simple, she taunted herself. She couldn't help it.

… … Karim's … … but … As
… … to the Riviera.
… … … … She … … be… Clod … … … … …
… when she didn't see him … a couple of days
… … on … … … … … and … …
… … … … … … … We … … …
… … answer was … … … … … … are
… … …

Chapter Nine

Karim had understated the forlorn grandeur of the jagged coastline. What Lindsay could see of it as they sped along the curved road was breathtaking, the view offering the occupants of the limousine glimpses of nature's spectacular beauty.

"Why didn't you tell me it was so beautiful? I'd have brought my camera."

"I can bring you back with your camera equipment if you want." A sidelong glance caught the nod of her head, the blond hair bouncing to and fro. "Late autumn is the best time for pictures. The stronger swells at that time of the year really churn up the sea."

"Good." And she wouldn't let him forget, either. Her thoughts were already diverted from her personal problems.

He took a right fork on to an unsealed road, and in seconds the car wheels were stirring up clouds of fine red dust. The road, if one could call the narrow goat track that, led to the sea and the shores of the Gulf of Oman. They drove through a small fishing village with a half dozen mud-brick, flat-roofed houses shuttered against the heat and seemingly devoid of life. Fishing nets hung drying on long poles, and in the sheltered bay several small boats, with eyes painted on the prows in Arabic tradition, bobbed up and down on the gentle swell.

"Where is everyone?" she asked curiously. There was no sign of life in the picturesque place, not even a prowling dog.

"Most likely in their cellars, resting. Like the workers at the desalination plant, they stay indoors during the heat of the day and come out when the tide is on the turn to fish, exchange gossip and make ready the evening meal."

"A sensible idea," she agreed and promptly wondered again why they were rattling around the land at this time of day. It was comfortable inside the limousine, but outside it certainly wouldn't be.

"We're almost there," he confided, taking another bend with ease.

Lindsay looked ahead, her eyes widening at the huge, yawning cave she saw dead ahead of them. "Does this place of yours have a name?" The question was facetious, for she had learned that Arabs loved to name anything and everything. A hill, a marketplace, a water fountain, a field where there had once been an ancient battle. Nothing of even the smallest note escaped this nationalistic fetish.

Getting her meaning, he laughed. "Of course. It is called the Remarkable Cave of the Prophet."

"That's a mouthful, but my personal favorite is the name of the well behind the El Zaihra Mosque in the city."

"I know it. The Well of the Fallen Woman's Tears. I presume you know the legend?"

"Yes, but the title says it all, doesn't it?"

"Mmmm...that's the edited version," he shot back. They laughed at the same time and, as always, the sound of her mellifluous tinkle erupting from her stirred his blood. He stopped the car where the road ended in the shade of some palms and swiveled about in the seat to study her. "I like your laugh, Lindsay Pentecost. Until I heard it the night you arrived at Shalima I had not realized how much such a sound had been missing from the palace. You have brought your own brand of happiness to all there, even to the staff."

"If I've helped, I'm glad," she said softly, her thoughts thrown out of kilter by his ability to catch her unawares with the things he spontaneously said.

"Let's explore. You will be amazed by this cave, I assure you," he promised. And in a sudden burst of energy, spurred by the need to be active lest he take her in his arms and kiss her till she begged for mercy, he opened the car door and stepped out.

As Lindsay alighted, a curious, faint, wailing sound assailed her ears. It sounded vaguely human and she cocked her head to one side trying to determine its source.

"The sound comes from deep in the cave, and with it comes a most amazing stream of cool air," he told her.

"Yes, I can feel it, but..." Instead of the blistering heat, a pleasant breeze was wafting from the cave's mouth, and because it was cool and moist there were clumps of plants, low wild shrubs and even several lush date palms. "I don't believe it," she said in a bemused tone, spreading her arms wide to catch the coolness. "It's incredible. How...?" She threw him a questioning look.

"No one knows for certain," he said with a casual shrug. "The best a scientific team came up with is that there's probably a huge underground cavern deep in the earth, and from a natural fault a pipeline that brings the air to the surface."

"It's wonderful. Miraculous," she enthused and then grinned cheekily at him. "Quite remarkable, in fact. I wish I'd brought my camera." He laughed at that, long and loud, and she watched in fascination as the strong columns at the sides of his throat corded with the effort. And with his hands at his lean hips and his feet planted solidly apart on the ground, he fitted the role of Arab sheikh to perfection. At once a tortuous spasm of desire raged through her, and to quell it she began scrambling toward the cave's mouth. When she'd gone several feet she looked back and teased him with his own words, "Come on, I want to explore this amazing place."

"You go ahead. I'll bring the picnic basket Tima packed and find a comfortable place for us to eat."

Half an hour later Karim cupped his hands to his mouth and called to Lindsay, whom he could see in the distance, "Are you hungry yet? You should have worked up an appetite with all that rock climbing."

His voice echoed loudly in the natural dome of the cave and she realized all of a sudden that, yes, she was hungry—and thirsty. She made her way back to him, chiding as she flopped down onto a corner of the rug where he sat cross-legged. "You're lazy, Karim El Hareembi. It's a very interesting place, this cave of yours."

"Remarkable, in fact," he parried back, a mischievous twinkle in his eye. "It's hardly mine though. I came here often as a boy, and I know the cave backward. I thought you'd enjoy pottering around by yourself. Besides, I didn't think it safe to leave the food unguarded."

"Hah." She snorted in mock disgust. "Who would dare steal anything from the mighty Sheikh of the Morasqs, First Minister of Cassar?"

His gaze fastened on her features—the green eyes sparkling with health, her cheeks rosily flushed from her exertions, the generous mouth now devoid of lipstick but, oh so ripe for kissing. Who indeed? "No one, of course, providing they know me." And, grinning devilishly, he pleaded, "May we eat now? I'm starving."

"Of course," she murmured. "Let's see what goodies Tima is tempting us with today."

"We must not forget the wine. I've had it cooling in the sea."

He strode to the water's edge, retrieved the bottle, and on the way back deftly popped the cork. "You'll have some, won't you? It's Beaujolais wine and it's wonderfully light and dry." When she nodded he filled both silver goblets that she held up to him.

They ate in silence, with obvious appreciation of the meal. Lindsay could feel the peace of the place surrounding her and wondered whether Karim was similarly affected. The cave itself was a phenomenon, and the man sitting cross-legged opposite her was just as remarkable. She sighed silently. Was it any wonder she'd been unable to stop herself from falling in love with him? He had all the qualities of the man of her dreams. He was magnificent, even when he was angry, and, she had to admit, a little scary, too.

She finished the last drop of wine, and as he refilled both their glasses, he said, "You've gone quiet all of a sudden. Tell me the thoughts running through that active brain of yours."

She almost choked on a mouthful of wine. She couldn't tell him her thoughts, so she said the first thing that came to her. "I . . . was wondering . . . why the people in the fishing village didn't settle closer to the cave? Wouldn't such a site be more pleasant for them?"

"There was an ancient settlement, but it was abandoned centuries ago. The present-day villagers treat the cave with reverence and hold a couple of religious festivals here by the sea, but otherwise they give the place a wide berth. Besides, in the winter the wind howls dreadfully through the cave, enough to frighten one witless, I believe."

Lindsay pushed her plate off her lap and stretched comfortably on the rug. Preceding her words with a yawn, she commented, "I should have been a cat instead of human. After food and that lovely wine all I want to do is sleep."

"Why don't you? We can stay as long as we like. In fact, I'm rather enjoying playing truant." His eyes slid over her slender form, and he added softly, "Maybe we should do this more often."

She removed her sunglasses, put them on top of the picnic basket, and looked across at him. "Sure you don't mind?" He shook his head, and she added, "I'll just have forty winks, no more. I promise."

"While you do I'll go and move the car into the shade," he said and walked away whistling softly. She was sound asleep when he returned with a small bag in one hand and two enormous multicolored beach towels over his shoulder. He stripped off his clothes until he was down to his trunks but, instead of heading for the sea, which had been his plan, he folded a towel, settled it beside her and sat down, cross-legged to watch her.

Relaxed in sleep and with her hair tumbled about her face she looked positively angelic. *Blanc infidèl* the souk traders called her, but with affection. In the past three months most Cassarians had grown used to her wandering around the city proper and the back streets, camera in hand and asking questions.

He never tired of looking at her, but he hadn't seen her in total repose before and was free to feast on her loveli-

ness. She had the milk-coffee tan he had known she would
acquire, and there was even an endearing dust of freckles
across her pert nose. His gaze moved down to her blouse,
the top button of which had come undone, and he glimpsed
the beginning soft swell of her firm, round breasts. He felt
the increasingly familiar ache in his loins and groaned. How
he ached to touch her, kiss her, to whisper of his passion for
her. With deep regret he dragged his gaze down the rest of
her slender, athletic form, the long shapely legs. Finally,
uttering a frustrated moan, he jumped up and sprinted to
the water.

He waded in until he was thigh deep, then plunged into
the salty depths, welcoming the initial chill needed to
dampen his ardor. He swam for a long time, trying to ex-
haust himself physically, to drain his need for her, but all
his thoughts led him back to Lindsay and to the contem-
plation of his feelings for her. She was special, he freely
admitted.

And one problem he could not deny was that he had to
exert patience and self-restraint over his emotions. This was
a first-time experience for him. In recent years there had
always been a ready supply of women whenever he'd felt
the physical need. And before, with Yasmin, the sweet wife
of his youth, who had been brought up in a strict Muslim
household where a man's word was law, his wishes were
considered above all else.

But Lindsay was, to use a cliché, a different kettle of fish.
He knew she desired him; she might even be a little infa-
tuated with him. But she was driven by an unreasonable
belief that because they came from different cultures a relationship between them was doomed to fail. Perhaps he
should fully relate to her the romantic story of his grandfather and grandmother. They, too, had experienced simi-

lar differences, yet had managed to overcome them and be happy.

And all at once he cursed the fact that he was leaving in three days on a round-the-world trip with the crown prince. If he had more days alone with her like this maybe she would learn to trust her feelings and to trust him. Yes, that was a goal he longed to achieve.

Lindsay woke with a start. Her eyes opened wide and widened some more as they encountered Karim sitting comfortably against a rock, naked except for his swimming trunks. For what seemed ages, though it was only seconds, her gaze was riveted on him. The bronzed chest, the muscled shoulders and powerful thighs. She felt the pounding of her heart, the blood pulsing through her veins till she thought they'd surely burst. He looked cool and relaxed, and suddenly she was on fire, burning with a need that only he could satisfy. And right now she had an overwhelming longing for him to do so.

She gulped down the lump in her throat and said in a reproachful tone, "You should have told me to bring my bathers."

He pointed to the small zip-up bag. "They're in there. I had Tima pack them."

"Great." She snatched the bag and looked for a place to change. Several yards away there was a clump of shoulder-high bushes that would give her some privacy. "Be back soon," she called over her shoulder as she hurried away. She returned in a few minutes wearing the same swimsuit she'd worn in the palace pool.

"How disappointing," he murmured huskily, letting his eyes rove over her with leisurely thoroughness. "I was praying for a brief bikini."

"I thought Arab men frowned on their women parading their . . . ahem . . . attributes." Too late she realized the slip of her tongue in implying that she was his woman.

"Not me. I think you'd look fantastic in a bikini."

She clucked her tongue in disgust and kicked sand over his feet. "Race you to the water," she challenged then promptly took off. She beat him and stopped at the water's edge, letting the sea lap around her ankles.

"It's not cold," he teased, and kicked water up onto her legs. When he saw her serious expression he asked, "What's wrong?"

"Oh, nothing." She saw his eyebrow lift questioningly and felt compelled to say, "I . . . it's just that I suddenly recalled what Udan said at the *wadi*. 'Beware the seashore.'" It was ridiculous, and probably meant nothing, but suddenly Lindsay felt cautious. "Perhaps I shouldn't go in."

"It's a perfectly safe place to swim. No rips, no undercurrents," Karim assured her. He, too, had forgotten the old man's warning. "Udan's predictions are not always correct, Lindsay, and besides, I am here to protect you." And before she could object or guess his intention he'd swung her up in his arms as effortlessly as he did the children and began wading into deeper water.

Her hands went around his neck automatically, but she wriggled against him in an effort to break free until she realized that the touch of his bare skin was igniting little fires of response throughout her body. She went very still and asked in a subdued tone, "W-will you put me down, Karim, please?"

"Sure." He began to lower her into the water an inch at a time, his grin broadening wickedly when she moaned in protest.

"You're a sadist," she accused, then laughed. Today he wasn't the Sheikh of the Morasqs nor she his children's tutor, but just a woman reveling in the company of the man she loved. And they were playing around like a couple of crazy teenagers. It was wonderful. She wished the day, and particularly this moment would never end.

"A sadist, am I?" he queried, his brows almost meeting in a frown of displeasure. "There's just no pleasing some women." He lifted her higher in his arms—level with his chest—and then threw her away from him into the water.

She came up spluttering and threatening, "I'll get you for that," at which he just laughed and swam away from her. Left to her own devices, she swam as far as the breaker line and then back till her feet touched bottom again. Determined to pay him back for ducking her, she dived under the water and swam up behind him.

On land she would have had no chance of pulling a man as big as Karim off balance, but in the water the weight difference wasn't as extreme. She caught him around the waist and pushed forward with her shoulder, causing him to lose his footing and go under. He tried to grab her, but she was too fast and sped out of reach, laughing heartlessly. He probably wouldn't like what she'd done, she thought gleefully, wading into the shallows. It had probably upset his masculine dignity. Thinking of that made her giggle. She half turned to see where he was and was promptly tackled and brought down with a thud on to her back in the surf and sand.

"Ouch," she yelled, the wind momentarily knocked out of her. Their bodies were tangled, with him lying half on top of her. "You brute," she said with feeling, "I bet you played rugby at Oxford."

"Yes, and I was a good fullback, too," he told her, his own breathing uneven but for a different reason.

"And so modest," she teased.

He lay atop her staring down, his black eyes burning with an intensity that made her shiver. His gaze roamed her face as the fingers of his right hand began to ease strands of wet hair from her cheeks and forehead. She must make him move somehow, so she could get away or she would not be responsible for her actions. A weakening languorousness was invading her limbs, steadily robbing her of the desire to do anything other than stay with him as they were now. But her vulnerability frightened her more, and in a desperate move she started to squirm again. "I...don't...th-think this is a g-good idea. You...you'd..." Her voice stilled as a sudden shiver of desire rose within her, engulfing her in a tidal wave of emotions—love, need, the desire to give all.

His gaze captured hers once more and held it. And as he stared into her depths seeking her very soul, all thinking on her part ceased. With a sigh, his lips came down to cover hers. It was a sweet, heart-rending kiss, almost reverent, and its very tenderness succeeded in finally destroying the control she'd been holding on to like an invisible lifeline. With a moan she gave up and kissed him back. She loved him, and just this once she would follow the dictates of her heart. Her arms, instead of pushing him away, clasped around his back and urged him even closer.

Her responsiveness unleashed emotions Karim had worked hard to contain. She was so sweetly giving, with the promise of a passion that matched his own. With a muffled groan he deepened their kiss, his tongue sliding between her lips, demanding conquest, receiving and mingling with her own. Supporting some of his weight on his elbows he let his long, hard length press her down into the wet sand until they were molded to each other in a way that left no doubt as to the needs of them both.

He wanted to explore more of her, and his hands began to caress her body. Quickly finding one breast he cupped it gently.

She sighed with delight, her fingers twining into his hair urging him on, and he was pleased to comply. In one deft movement he slipped the costume strap from her shoulder and trailed sweet kisses across her breast. Lindsay thought she would burst from the feelings he aroused. He nudged her legs apart and positioned himself so that she could feel his throbbing manhood scorching and branding her, and the empty ache inside her multiplied.

"Dear, sweet Lindsay, you are driving me out of my mind with desire. Are you aware of the power you have over me? I can't think of anyone or anything but you. My nights are filled with dreams of you in my arms, of making love till we are exhausted..." His lips trailed an upward path to claim her mouth again.

"It's...the same for me," she whispered. Didn't he know that? Wasn't her uninhibited response enough for him to see that she wanted what he wanted? She ached for his kisses, yearned for his hands to touch her everywhere and take her to the paradise of which he had once spoken. And so she drew his face down to hers and kissed him with unrestrained passion.

Both came up gasping for air. As Lindsay's lids fluttered open she saw something in Karim's liquid black depths that instantly chilled her heated blood. Masculine triumph accentuated by passion was mirrored there. The small part of her mind that was still capable of coherent thought realized her love for him was pushing her to the brink. She was about to surrender completely to his will.

She blinked in astonishment and dismay. The words that had been drummed into her since puberty came back to haunt her: Sex without commitment was wrong. But, she argued, she loved him, didn't she? And didn't that make it right? Yes. No! Not if Karim didn't feel the same commitment. Not if she was just another conquest to him.

"Karim, no. I don't want to..." She breathed the words, but they were a lie. She desperately wanted release from the emotional torture they were putting each other through. She wanted that very much. Only...only...her conscience was already sending out messages why she shouldn't. Don't make the biggest mistake in your life, it told her. You risk losing your identity if you allow him to rule supreme over you. He'll own you body and soul. And remember, the emir wants him to remarry, and when he does he'll discard you for his bride. The thought of him in another woman's arms made her almost cry out in despair and her "No!" was torn from her heart.

Finally her plea got through to him, and though his features mirrored disbelief, he rolled away from her.

Karim sat up and bent his knees to his chest and clasped them with his arms. He was nonplussed—and angry—at the way she had divorced herself from her feelings. Could she really turn them on and off so easily? He couldn't, as his uneven breathing and still-pounding heart attested to. He needed to know why she had gone cold on him.

He reached across to her and placed his hand on her smooth thigh and felt the muscle tense at his touch. "What is the matter, Lindsay? Tell me what you are afraid of."

A few minutes earlier he thought he had succeeded in getting her to put her fears away and to be the warm responsive woman he knew she could be. Now he wasn't sure, for she continued to confound him with her mercurial mood changes.

With some embarrassment Lindsay adjusted her costume strap and willed herself to stare pointedly at his hand till he removed it from her thigh. She dredged up the presence of mind to say, "It isn't . . . right." And that was all. Though the words sounded lame and meaningless to her, she convinced herself that the only way it would be right was if he loved her as she loved him . . . and she knew he didn't!

"Not right?" he echoed. His gaze narrowed to slits, and he regarded her in stony silence for a moment, though it seemed much longer. "Why?" he asked coldly. "Am I not good enough for you?" There was a thousand years of Arabian pride in the upward tilt of his chin. "Is it the difference in our skin tones?"

"No!" she cried out, shocked that he could even think it might be that.

"What then?"

She was suddenly struck dumb. How could she tell him she was afraid? If she did he would surely discover how deeply she cared, and she would be bound to him forever. "I'm afraid . . ." she began, intending to continue and say something eminently English and sensible.

He pounced on that and shot the question at her. "Of me?"

"N-no I . . . I . . ." Oh, damn! She was stammering like a nervous fifth-grader again. "N-not of you personally. Of . . . if . . . I mean, of the relationship failing . . ." There, she had got it out, off her chest, so to speak, but she didn't feel better. She felt dreadful, and admitting her fears only added to her growing misery.

"In life, some things worth having carry a risk, Lindsay," he said simply. "We of the desert tribes have lived that philosophy for centuries."

"It's impossible. We're so different. Our backgrounds, our lifestyles, our personalities . . ."

At such an admission from her he threw back his head and gave a short laugh. "These things mean nothing, my angel. Nothing. It is what we feel inside for each other that counts. All else can be dealt with, believe me, trust me," he finished in his most persuasive tone.

She waited, hoping he'd elaborate, hoping he would declare that he cared for her as she did for him, but when he said nothing she hardened her heart. She had fallen under the spell of that silken tongue of his before and this time her sanity, her ability to function even, depended on not being similarly swayed. "I don't agree," she said quietly, but as positively as she could. "In the end we'd drift apart." As most relationships do when governed by physical passion alone. "Now, I think . . . please, can we drop the subject?" She looked toward the horizon where the sun, a fiery red ball, was beginning to set. "Isn't it time we thought about leaving? It's a long drive back to Cassar."

Karim's hand balled into a fist, and he thumped the wet sand in frustration. He had never known a woman with the strength of will that Lindsay Pentecost exhibited. It was not natural for a woman to be so strong, he was sure. He was used to the opposite sex bending to his will, not opposing it as she did. Before, she had almost melted in his arms with a desire that had matched his, and at which he'd been delighted. But equal to her passion was her resolve and, in spite of his disappointment and a mounting sense of frustration, he found himself admiring her as a worthy, if misguided, adversary.

How could he convince her that her fears were unfounded, that he trusted her completely and was more than a little hurt that such a feeling was not reciprocated? And he knew that opposites attracted—had they not done so since Adam and Eve? Just as he knew that the affection between them would grow and deepen with the passage of time. Aaahh, but he knew he could not convince her, even with all his verbal skills. It was something she had to learn for herself.

His mind harked back to the fact that she did not trust him, and he wondered why. Surely she didn't think he would ever hurt her? He was a man of honor in all things of importance, and she, he confessed, was very important to him. In his confusion he could not hold back the sarcastic taunt, and as he rose in a fluid, graceful movement from the wet sand, he lashed out, "As there seems little purpose in remaining, we might as well leave. But—" he paused, considered his phrasing and then said in a solemn tone "—be warned, Lindsay. One day you will come to me of your own free will, and there will be no constraints between us ever again."

Wincing at his curtness, Lindsay watched him walk away, and her heart slowly broke into a thousand pieces. What was the matter with her? Was she crazy? She loved the sheikh, really loved him, yet she was afraid to risk all. What an emotional coward she must be. Was it any wonder he'd shown his disgust? Karim was so strong, so sure of himself and his role in life and his future. And she . . . what joy did her future hold if he now despised her?

She stood up, but anguish made her legs buckle, and she dropped to her knees in the sand. Had she just made the biggest mistake in her life? Oh God, had she?

Slowly, and with her shoulders drooping dejectedly, she picked herself up and followed the trail he had made in the sand, trudging back to the picnic spot where he was already packing up.

Chapter Ten

Reclining on a lounger, shaded by a multicolored umbrella, Lindsay made sure her peripheral vision surreptitiously covered the children playing on the beach. The boys had conned Sonja into letting them bury her in the sand and were happily piling bucketfuls of the material onto a patient, slowly disappearing Sonja. The girl had a sweet, pleasant nature, Lindsay thought and was somehow reminded of Blaise, her half sister who was five years younger than the twins. With her bright auburn hair and blue eyes, Blaise, being tomboyish and with a firebrand temper, was Sonja's opposite in nature. She wouldn't, she knew, take half the nonsense the boys dished out to Sonja.

She sighed, and the familiar feeling of depression settled over her. In two days they were leaving this heavenly place, Karim's magnificent villa on the Riviera, and she wouldn't be sorry.

To say that this had been the most miserable six weeks of her life was an understatement, though to all who saw her she probably looked as if she'd been having a ball. There had been sight-seeing excursions aplenty, shopping sprees at glamorous boutiques and visits to the casinos in Monte Carlo with Shareel and Monna. She had attended innumerable parties to please Karim's sister-in-law, who had tried unsuccessfully to pair her off with several bachelors. But the fun, the glamour and the activity hadn't impressed Lindsay because the one person who would have made it all perfect—Karim—wasn't there to share it with her.

She hadn't thought it possible to miss anyone as much as she missed him. She even missed their regular spats and that imperious, commanding tone of his, the sound of which could make her heart flutter. She could die, she suddenly realized, from this love of hers; that's how miserable she felt. And there was no respite from it. She thought about him all day and dreamed about him all night. Her appetite had practically vanished, and it was becoming an effort to carry on the most mundane conversation with anyone.

In six weeks she'd had lots of time to think, and at the ripe old age of twenty-four she had discovered something about herself that had previously escaped her. She wanted to be happy. And the only thing that would make her happy—ecstatically so—would be to be with the sheikh. She no longer cared about the differences between them: he had said they could work it out, and she believed that if Karim said they could, well, they could. She trusted him that much. Love and trust... the two went hand in hand, didn't they? And Karim was a sensitive, honest, perfectly trustworthy man.

She didn't care that the emir wanted him to remarry. She would take whatever happiness was offered to her and beyond that she refused to contemplate. Her change in attitude was a total surprise. She had always prided herself on her logic and common sense, but they didn't seem impor-

tant now. The only thing of importance was her love for the
sheikh—who wanted to give her so much. She felt a slow,
melting warmth flood through her as she recalled their
lovemaking. He was everything she wanted. And if he still
wanted her when he returned to Cassar...well...next time
she wouldn't fight him off.

It took little time for life in Shalima Palace to return to
normal, and just as quickly the children were grumbling
about schoolwork. The sheikh seemed busier than ever and
more remote than he had in the first days after Lindsay's
arrival. At times she wondered if she had fantasized the
sensual interlude between them on the sand near the Remarkable Cave. Her feelings weren't imaginary; they were
painfully real. But Karim was so distant and formal to her
now, and since their return he made sure that when they
were in the same room together they were never alone.

At the dinner table the fifth night after their return from
the villa, Karim watched Lindsay push the food around on
her plate and eat little of it. Everyone at the table was
chatting normally and no one except him seemed to notice
how withdrawn she was. He had purposely kept away from
her since their return, feigning the pressure of work.
Though not seeing her, touching her or hearing her voice
for six long weeks had almost driven him out of his mind.

She, too, he noted, had suffered during the separation.
She was pale and had lost several pounds. Not enough to
make her thin, just a touch ethereal, which only added to
her loveliness. And anyway, he decided, it was right that she
should suffer. She was the one keeping them apart. But not
for much longer, he hoped as his dark gaze roamed her
features hungrily. She looked—from the pensive, appealing glances she occasionally intercepted—as if she were
rapidly approaching some kind of decision. Silently he

willed her to make that decision soon, for more than once he had regretted the vow he'd made that day at the Remarkable Cave that she would have to come to him. The remnants of his patience were being tested sorely by her unwillingness to accept that kismet had ordained their union even before they'd met.

He watched her push her virtually untouched plate away and smiled grimly to himself. *Aahhh, my angel, this state between us cannot be borne for much longer. We both need, want, a satisfactory resolution desperately.*

Across the table Lindsay felt the sheikh's gaze on her and from beneath her lashes swept him a sly glance. He could be so...intimidating, so unbelievably attractive and so distant! Everything between them seemed to have gone wrong and it was, she admitted, mostly her fault. Her idiotic fear of forming a relationship, plus their six-week separation, had apparently led to a cooling-off in his affection. But her own inner tension was worsening with each day that passed. She couldn't eat or sleep properly and even her ability to ably teach the children was becoming impaired. She felt that she was in a no-man's-land of unrequited love. Tears began to well under her eyelids and she furiously blinked them away. Eager to escape the sheikh's curious, penetrating gaze, she excused herself and left the dinner table.

But once alone in her quarters Lindsay was unable to relax. The tension inside her was becoming unbearable. She could think of nothing but Karim and her feelings for him, and she knew she would have no peace until things were sorted out. He now seemed distant to her, and she agonized over the reason. Could a man's feelings, desires, change that dramatically in six weeks? Had the separation made him realize that Yasmin, his late wife, still held sway over his heart? Or, perhaps the emir had already requested the sheikh to remarry. The thought sent her heart spiraling downward.

In agitation she paced the tiled floor, and after half an hour's continuing restlessness she made a decision. She had to know where she stood with Karim or she would go crazy!

In the bathroom she checked her appearance in the mirror and practiced a confident smile. From her desk she took the folder containing the children's monthly school reports, tucked it under her arm and headed to where she was certain to find Karim at this time of the evening. Walking along the corridor she only just managed to quell her nervousness by smoothing her white skirt and fiddling with the collar of her rose-pink silk blouse. She pushed a rebellious blond lock from her forehead before tapping several times on the intricate carving of the arabesque door to his office.

Inside, Karim stood by the long window staring out at the floodlit garden. He spun around as the knocking shattered his thoughts and called imperiously, "Come."

As soon as he recognized the intruder, his pulse leaped erratically. She had finally come to him! He watched her approach, sensing her nervousness, and to put her at ease gently requested, "Please, Lindsay, do sit down. You are a most pleasant interruption." Not that he'd been working anyway, he confessed to himself. His thoughts had been, as usual, centered on the lovely, but maddening creature presently seating herself before him.

"Thank you. I—" she paused, trying to gather her courage "—brought the children's reports. Y-you might want to read through them before . . . deciding on which boarding school you wish to send Ali and Darius to in the spring."

"That was thoughtful of you," he said, taking the report from her as he came around the desk. "But when the time comes for a decision I am certain we will all need to be together to discuss such an important matter.''

She watched him sit on the marble-topped desk and casually arrange the folds of his linen caftan about his splendid physique. Her gaze focused fascinatedly on the extravagantly large, state ruby ring and, suddenly, the closeness of him caused all cohesive thought to flee. What was she going to say, and how could she introduce the subject of ''them'' without dying of embarrassment?

She took a deep breath and tentatively began, ''Ummm...we...have not had much time t-to...'' Oh she wished he'd stop staring at her so intensely, the look was completely scattering her wits. ''Discuss anything... since you returned from your trip....''

''I know,'' he agreed. ''Was there some particular subject you wanted to talk over with me?'' he asked with a seemingly innocent smile.

Wretch! He knew full well what particular subject she meant, as was evidenced by the wicked gleam in his dark eyes. He was actually enjoying her discomfort. But perhaps she deserved it. After all, wasn't she the one who'd been too timid to acknowledge that what they felt for each other was special? All right, she conceded grimly, he deserved his little victory.

''About us,'' she murmured, and then the words came out all in a tumble. ''Things cannot continue between us as they presently are. I can't concentrate on my work with the children, on anything. I need to know... Is there? Do you...?'' There was so much she wanted, needed to know. About his feelings. If in fact, he still wanted her? About Emir Abdullah's plans for him to remarry—had Cassar's ruler been serious? And... about Yasmin? Where did she stand... on... everything. But somehow all her thoughts became muddled, and all that came out was a disjointed plea. "About Yasmin? I know you loved her deeply. Have you, do you . . . ?"

"Still mourn her?" he finished for her, compassion for her anxious state finally triumphing. He stood up, reached down and pulled her up out of the chair so that they faced each other. "My dear, I sense that active brain of yours has many questions, and I will be pleased to answer them as best I can. Yes, I can say in truth that I am over my loss. But Yasmin's memory will always hold a special place in my heart. That is only fitting. She was my wife, my first love and the mother of my children. However—" his black eyes roamed her features, their study of her as eloquent as a caress "—thanks to you, Lindsay, I have accepted the tragedy of her untimely death and appeased my guilt."

Lindsay swallowed the sudden lump in her throat, her gaze transfixed on his face as she murmured softly, "What do you mean?"

"Life is for living, and I know she would want me to be happy." And, my sweet one, he added silently, I intend to be just that, with you.

"I-I'm glad. I thought..." What had she thought? That Yasmin's ghost would remain between them forever? Yes. Suddenly she wanted to tell him everything that was in her heart. That he held her life, her future in his hands to do with as he willed. "Karim, I want to tell you . . ." But then the shrill ring of the desk phone brought her sentence to an abrupt halt.

Karim sighed loudly at the interruption. His hand caressed her cheek fleetingly as he said, "One moment." He picked up the handset and barked impatiently into it. "Yes?"

Lindsay watched the frown burrow across his forehead and saw his sharp, hawkish features set into serious lines.

Something, she knew instinctively, was very wrong. She could tell by the stiff, alert way he now held himself.

"Yes. Yes! Tell the emir I will go immediately." He banged the handset down but had the grace to bestow a rueful smile on her as he punched the button for Shareel's extension and said rapidly, "Shareel, get the limousine. There is an emergency at the oil refinery. No, I don't know precisely what it is but the emir needs us there—now."

He turned back to Lindsay, and when he spoke his tone was regretful. "I must go," he told her. He kissed the back of her hand in a tender, apologetic gesture, then strode purposefully toward the door. Opening it, he paused only long enough to take in her startled expression of dismay and say, "When I return we will conclude this conversation, Lindsay. That's a promise." And then he was gone.

Lindsay blinked in amazement, torn between the need to physically vent her frustration by hurling something at the closed door or to laugh hysterically and ease the tension inside her. Minutes before she had very nearly had an anxiety attack worrying over what she'd been going to tell him—all to no avail. She expelled a sigh, thrust her hands deep into the slitted pockets of her cotton skirt and wondered if she and Karim were ever destined to resolve their problems.

She retraced her steps to her quarters and latched on to one positive thought. At least she knew that he had put Yasmin's memory to rest. That was something, wasn't it?

The spring in Lindsay's step was noticeably light as she walked across the fountain courtyard, acknowledging with a smile the guards respectful salutes as they opened the doors for her, allowing her to move into the palace foyer.

Beneath her arm was a wrapped bundle, her latest purchase from the souk, and she would wear it tonight. The soft wool lemon caftan with its gold thread embroidery around the neck, sleeves and hemline had been made for her by one of the most skillful seamstresses in the bazaar. And, even if she said so herself, she looked fabulous in it.

She knew that Karim and Shareel were still at the oil refinery but were expected home in the evening. Tonight she and the sheikh would conclude the discussion that had been interrupted last night. She smiled dreamily, conspiratorially, and amended her thoughts. Discussion wasn't exactly all she had in mind. She hoped, intended, the evening would culminate in something much more exciting than a conversation between them. Yes, indeed!

Suddenly the silence of the palace struck her as odd. She wondered where the children were. Ali, she knew, was ill with a slight fever; but where were the other three? She opened the playroom door and found Hisham playing alone with a pile of brightly colored blocks.

"Hello, Hisham. That looks like fun." She dropped to her haunches and helped him to steady a wobbling tower. "Where are the twins?" she casually asked.

"Gone," he said and carried on with his project.

"Gone where?"

"Just gone," he said again, this time sparing her a brief glance before returning his concentration to the task at hand.

He clearly didn't know where they were but Lindsay, having some experience of Darius's pranks, frowned. She stood up, pressed the servants bell and within seconds Tima appeared.

"Have you seen the twins, Tima?"

"No, Miss Lindsay, not for an hour or so. They came to the kitchen for something to eat, then said they were going to their rooms to rest." The middle-aged housekeeper's expression began to show concern. "Is something wrong?"

"I don't know. But I have a feeling..." Lindsay murmured half to herself.

They left Hisham to his own devices and retreated to the corridor outside. "You search downstairs and the grounds, while I do upstairs," Lindsay ordered and, climbing the staircase, she tried to ignore the queasy feeling in her stomach.

Ten minutes later Tima met her on the staircase landing. She was wringing her hands convulsively, her features creased with worry. "Oh, Miss Lindsay, their horses are missing."

"I'm not surprised. Their riding gear isn't in their rooms, either."

"Oh, dear. What will His Excellency say? They're only supposed to go riding with him, or with you."

"Yes, well, His Excellency won't be back until later tonight. If we can find the imps and bring them back he won't have to know straightaway. I'll devise a suitable chastisement for them myself." Anxiety was setting in. What was worse, she had no idea in which direction they'd gone.

"I don't understand how they got out the palace gates unnoticed," Tima said.

"I don't, either," Lindsay responded, then the answer came to her. "They probably sneaked through when the afternoon guards were changing over." Tima nodded in agreement.

Lindsay tried to think as a child might if planning an escapade. Neither Darius nor Sonja would want to get caught. They probably planned to return before dinner, so that meant they couldn't go too far. But, and she pondered hard, where and why, and in which direction? There were at least three to choose from, and as she couldn't cover them alone she would have to enlist the help of the palace guards. That wasn't a problem because the sheikh's staff

were devoted to all the children and would do anything to
see them safely returned to the palace.

Tima's thoughts were clearly in line with her own because she said, "One of the guards mentioned to Darius
that he'd seen a small freighter on the beach. Its rudder was
broken in a storm, and it ran aground last week."

Yes! That would have sparked Darius's love of adventure and his innate curiosity. And he would have had no
trouble in enlisting Sonja's company. She adored her dominating twin and looked for any excuse to ride her beloved
pony, Shalimar.

"Where, Tima?"

Tima frowned, trying to remember. "The coastline north
of the city. Near the peninsula, I think."

The two women exchanged meaningful glances.

"Isn't that where...the Sheikha had her accident?"
Lindsay asked, but she already knew the answer. A shiver
of foreboding ran down her spine. The sheikh had expressly forbidden that particular piece of coastline to the
children, and even she, for once, had adhered to his wishes
and not explored the area.

But...if Karim found out. She swallowed the tightness
in her throat and knew she would not like to witness his
fury. It would be frightening to behold. So, in rapid stac-
cato sentences she fired orders at the housekeeper.

"Have guards search south of the city, the old quarter
and the bazaar. Have others drive toward the Wadi of Sinjin. They must ask anyone they meet, diplomatically of
course, if they've seen the sheikh's children. Oh, yes, have
them issued with walkie-talkies from the ordinance section
so you can monitor their progress, and ask Monna to help
you. I will search toward the peninsula. Have a servant
saddle Diablo...."

"But he is the sheikh's horse and very spirited."

"And fleet of foot, Tima. We need speed if we are to find those children and return them to the palace before the sheikh returns."

"Yes, of course." Tima demurred to Lindsay's authority as if it came directly from the sheikh himself and lumbered off to carry out her commands.

In her quarters Lindsay hurriedly changed into cotton slacks and shirt. She grabbed a broad-brimmed hat, and almost as an afterthought she picked up the woolen desert cape she wore whenever she rode, knowing that when the sun set the night would turn noticeably chilly. With her features set in taut, grim lines, she headed to the stables.

Lindsay raced through the old quarter, which was the shortest route to the shoreline, but it took longer than usual because Cassarians were out in force shopping and trading. The women gossiped in groups, while the men sat at tables in open cafés protected from the sun by draped awnings, drinking coffee or sweetened tea in small glasses as they played dominoes or backgammon.

When she reached the shoreline Lindsay took care. She dismounted and led Diablo down the rocky path where Yasmin had fallen to her death. But once on the sand she remounted and galloped at close to breakneck speed along the beach for what seemed miles before sighting the beached freighter in the distance. Getting closer she could see the children and loudly sighed with relief. They were safe. But they wouldn't be quite so carefree after she'd given them a talking-to. They were thoughtless little horrors and would pay dearly for their naughtiness. She reined Diablo in hard and jumped to the sand. The children, absorbed in their adventure, weren't aware of her presence.

Sonja saw her first. "Miss Lindsay!"

Then Darius, on the freighter deck, leaned over the railing. Immediately his features took on a guilty look, and he echoed his sister's surprise. "Miss Lindsay."

"Come down, Darius. At once," Lindsay ordered in her best no-nonsense tone.

He obediently scampered down the rope ladder and came to stand beside his sister, his hangdog caught-out expression almost comical.

"What do you have to say for yourselves? You know that what you've done is inexcusable, don't you?" She tried her best to sound really angry with them, but the long ride and only just managing to control Karim's spirited stallion, plus finding them safe, had drained away most of the anger. Just momentarily, she silently promised them. The palace would be a better place to give them a thorough dressing down.

Darius kicked at an imaginary sand pile and muttered with a touch of his old rebelliousness. "No one was supposed to find out where we were. And we were going to be back before you or anyone else missed us."

Lindsay glanced pointedly at her watch and stared hard at him. "I don't know how you were going to manage that, young man," she said archly. "It's only an hour to your supper time which, I think, this evening you'll both be missing."

Sonja sighed resignedly. "We...kind of forgot about the time, didn't we, Darius?"

"I guess so," he agreed and kicked the sand mutinously again.

Lindsay almost dropped her stern mask and smiled. He looked so much like his father. But then, thinking of Karim made her remember his imminent return and that other parties were looking for them. She took the walkie-talkie out of the saddlebag and started broadcasting to Tima that she had found them by the peninsula. There was a lot of static and crackling on the line because of the distance from the palace and the cliffs close by, and she wasn't sure that Tima heard the transmission. She just had to hope she did.

"Well, believe me we will discuss it all thoroughly back at the palace. But now, pack up your belongings. We'll ride back immediately," she ordered in a tone that brooked no debate.

While they packed up the picnic items and the blanket they'd sat on Lindsay glanced out to sea and noticed something peculiar. The on-shore breeze, a pleasantly cool one, had suddenly died, and in its place a stillness, apart from the noisy surf, pervaded. And the sky above, cloudless as usual, was darkening prematurely. It made her think that she didn't want to be far from the city's lights when night came.

"It's still all of a sudden, Darius. I wonder why?" she said to the young boy.

He looked up and glanced around him, and a tight expression came over his youthful features. "It is an omen, I think."

"Of what?"

"I'm not sure. A change in the weather, possibly. If... only I could—" he paused and his forehead knotted in a frown "—recall what Papa said about..."

"Perhaps it means it will be cooler tomorrow," Sonja put in hopefully.

"I don't think so." Her twin's doubts dashed her hopes. "But... I remember now, Miss Lindsay, the sign—" he moved in sudden agitation, grabbing his tutor's arm. "We must hurry back to the palace," he said and began pulling her toward the tethered horses.

"Why? What is it? Tell me, Darius."

"It's a *kaus*," the boy said, already able to see its rapid approach. He pointed to the peninsula where the heat haze had given way to a dark mass of cloud, swirling and growing and darkening the features of the shoreline. "A desert sandstorm is coming, we must hurry. Believe me, it is not something to be caught in."

Lindsay didn't need to be told twice. The three of them sprinted to the horses and mounted up, and as they did she was reminded of Udan's prediction. *Beware the seashore.* His words ran through her mind again and again. This was the danger the old soothsayer had seen when he'd read her palm many weeks ago.

"Put your cloak on, Miss Lindsay," Sonja advised, pulling her own cloak plus a scarf from her saddlebag.

They galloped along the beach with Lindsay in the lead on Diablo. But long before they reached the rocky path she looked back at the approaching reddish-yellow cloud and knew, fatalistically, that they couldn't outrun it. Their best chance was to find shelter and dig in till it had passed.

She then recalled, with nail-biting clarity, being caught in a recent sandstorm in Cassar's marketplace. In minutes the features of the souk had been obliterated by particles of red dust that stung unbearably and had clogged her nose and mouth and hurt her eyes. It had been a harrowing experience, but she'd been fortunate in that one of the traders had seen her and dragged her into his shop and banged the roller shutter down tight. And there they had sat, cross-legged on the dirt floor, drinking tea and talking for two hours until the storm had passed.

But here there was no shelter or help.

"We can't outrun the storm, children. We'd best try to find a place to sit it out."

Darius, manfully trying to hide his fear, asked the obvious. "Where?"

Lindsay bit her lip and tried to concentrate. Yes, where? The freighter! She looked back again to see that it had already been swallowed up by the storm. Around them there wasn't any place even remotely suitable, except a cluster of medium-sized boulders. "There." She pointed to them. "They'll have to do," she said and urged her mount toward them.

"We'll dig in behind the rocks and use the horses as a shield. Our cloaks will protect us a little, too. Come on, we haven't any time to waste."

"Oh, Miss Lindsay, I am afraid...." Sonja whimpered, coming abreast of her in the saddle. "Sandstorms kill people."

"Well, this one won't kill us. It might make us a bit uncomfortable but that's all it will do," she assured the youngster with what she hoped was a suitable show of courage. Then with feverish speed they dismounted. She and Darius began to hollow out a shallow trench while Sonja held the horses' reins. But, agitated by the approaching storm Sonja's mount broke free and galloped off.

"It doesn't matter," Lindsay soothed Sonja. "She'll head for the palace. Just hold tight to Midnight and Diablo. Better still, get them down on their haunches." Gritting her teeth against the particles of sand beginning to sting her face, she organized the horses as near to the trench as she could. She tore strips off the bottom of her cloak to cover the horses' eyes so they wouldn't be afraid and then went about the task of settling herself and the twins in the trench. She threw the cloaks over them, covering the edges with sand, and lastly she lay down, too, her back acting as a sort of shield for the two children.

The sandstorm raged and shrieked furiously for hours. If she'd thought her earlier experience at the souk was bad, it paled to insignificance compared with what they were now being subjected to. Strong gusts of wind and sand battered her flimsily protected body mercilessly, and the limited air space soon became suffocatingly hot. Everything was made worse by the fact that she couldn't shut off her thoughts. She kept thinking the most morbid things, especially what Sonja had said—*sandstorms kill people.* What if it . . .

No! She wouldn't, couldn't allow herself to give in to such thoughts and, stubbornly, her lips compressed together. She couldn't give up. She and the twins had too much to live for.

But it became the most petrifying, miserable, dirty and uncomfortable few hours she'd ever experienced.

When the storm finally abated and everything was still again, they extricated themselves from the sandy mound that had half-buried them and saw it was pitch dark. The horses, too, were glad it was over, whinnying and nuzzling at their riders affectionately till they were petted.

"We can't attempt to make our way back till first light," Lindsay said sensibly.

That was the last straw for Sonja. Overcome by the trauma she burst into tears, and it took all of Lindsay's calming skills and young Darius's words of comfort to ease the girl's fears.

To make the time pass Lindsay talked and talked about many things and her family in particular. She related stories of her half sister, Blaise, until finally exhaustion overtook the children and they fell asleep.

But similar rest didn't come to Lindsay. She thought of Karim and wished he were with them. He would have known exactly what to do. But she contented herself with the knowledge that at daylight he would find them and then they would all be truly safe.

She even welcomed the thought of his wrath and knew he would be mightily displeased by his offsprings' misadventure. But she hoped he wouldn't be too angry. They had all been subjected to a terrible fright and surely that was punishment enough.

Chapter Eleven

Karim's return to Shalima Palace coincided with the on-slaught of the seasonal sandstorm, which had first hit the peninsula and then moved on to engulf the city of Cassar. It fell to Tima, chief housekeeper at the Palace and long-time retainer to the sheikh, to relay the news that the twins and Lindsay were missing. And it was fortunate that she could tell him that she'd received a garbled communication that Lindsay had found the children, so they knew exactly where the trio could be found.

The sheikh knew he couldn't mount a rescue mission until the sandstorm moved on—to do so at its height would put more people in danger. Like a man possessed he stalked the palace's corridors moving restlessly like a caged panther, scanning the windows for evidence of the storm's abatement. He'd issued orders to Shareel and the guards that two of the emir's helicopters were to be put on alert and ready to take off as soon as a change in the weather allowed.

As the minutes passed, Karim's anguish and level of frustration multiplied due to his feeling of complete helplessness and having to bow, if only temporarily, to the forces of nature.

But, if anything positive was gleaned from his forced stay in the palace, it came as he relived the past three months of his life—the length of time Lindsay had been the children's tutor. What an enormous change she had brought to the palace, to the children and, greatest of all, to him. He stopped pacing before the office window as something, a realization, came to him in a sharp burst of enlightenment. He loved Lindsay Pentecost. Yes, yes, he loved her! Distractedly he ran a sinewed hand through his already disheveled mane of black hair and was confounded as to why he had not recognized the emotion before tonight. She had irritated him, argued with him, often had driven him to distraction and finally... she enchanted him, utterly. The muscle in his jaw flexed, and he made a silent vow that when he found the twins and her he would never, ever, let her go.

Suddenly in the midst of his thoughts his senses registered a lessening in the sandstorm's ferocity, and that galvanized him into action. He called to Shareel, "Tell the copter pilots to warm up the engines. We will take off within the next fifteen minutes. Sooner if the wind drops faster."

Lindsay had lost all track of time. They could have been surrounded by darkness for one, two or even three hours, she just couldn't tell. She also wished she could sleep as the twins were, but the continual pounding of the waves, the stress caused by the sandstorm, and being outdoors all combined to keep her awake. She felt deathly tired, drained and thought longingly of the cool sheets and her divan's softness back at the palace.

In the darkness she heard a strange noise somewhere, but far away. She looked up the coastline to where she could see, dimly, the glow of Cassar's city lights. And there, moving slowly toward them with their navigational lights blinking and searchlights splayed in a wide circle on the ground, were two helicopters.

It was Karim, she would stake her life on it. Thank God!

The whirring sounds became deafening and woke Sonja and Darius, who clambered to their feet and stood, one on either side of their tutor, watching the aircraft approach until the three of them were illuminated by powerful beams as bright as daylight itself.

The moment the helicopters landed Karim and Shareel, followed closely by two of the palace guards, ran toward them.

"Lindsay...children."

Smiling, Lindsay watched under the powerful beams of light as Darius and Sonja charged into their father's outstretched arms. It was a beautiful sight to behold, she admitted with a lump in her throat, just seeing the sheikh visibly moved by the happy occurrence of finding his children unharmed.

And over the tops of their small heads Karim stared at Lindsay as if he were really seeing her for the first time. And when he spoke, his relieved tone belied the sternness of his words. "The worry you have put me and the emir through. The entire household has been unable to rest."

"We're sorry, Papa. We didn't mean to," a shamefaced Darius appealed to his father. "Miss Lindsay, she knew what to do when the sandstorm came." And he went on to relate to his father, Shareel and the guards the events that had befallen the three of them.

Karim's steadfast gaze remained on Lindsay as Darius, with Sonja's help, told him what had happened. His only comment when they were done was a quiet, "Did she now? You must tell me everything again when we get back to Shalima." He turned and barked an order at one of the guards. "Radio back that we've found them and that they seem unharmed. But have Dr. Farouk waiting at the palace to check them when we return."

"At once, Excellency." The taller guard nodded, saluted and raced back to one of the helicopters.

"Shareel, take Sonja and Darius to the first copter. Make them comfortable," the sheikh commanded. "I'll attend to Lindsay myself and follow. The sooner we get them to the palace the better I'll like it."

Shareel obeyed instantly. Although Lindsay was overwhelmed with exhaustion and relief, she stood her ground, immobilized by the sheikh's presence. She longed to fall into his arms, but he looked so stern and sounded so angry that confusion won, and in the end she remained silent, waiting for a sign that his anger was not directed at her.

Karim moved toward her, his strong arms going around her shoulders to support her as he offered her a canteen of water. "Are you all right, Lindsay? Drink," he commanded.

"Yes, I'm fine." The statement was something of an exaggeration as she felt utterly fatigued.

He stared down at her, his thoughts harking back several hours to the revelation that had come to him. There was much he wanted to say to her. To thank her and to tell her of his love, but what came out was a tense, "What am I to do with all of you? You have caused me . . . much trouble, much alarm."

She knew he meant the twins mostly and rushed to their defense. "I know they were naughty to do what they did,

Karim, but . . . I think this experience has been punishment enough.''

"Do you now?" he queried. "I do not necessarily agree that you are the best judge in this matter. However, there will be time enough back at the palace to discuss the matter thoroughly."

Ignoring her mild cry of protest he lifted her up in his arms and strode toward the aircraft. "You've all been through a terrible ordeal, but you'll feel much better once we get you some medical attention. Rest now," he told her and smiled as she gratefully laid her head against his chest.

Karim tenderly lifted her into the helicopter. But he controlled the urge, with some difficulty, to kiss and caress away the tiredness and anxiety he saw in her face. There would be a more fitting time to reveal his feelings to Lindsay Pentecost, the woman who had brought the glory of love into his life again. Tonight he had almost lost her and the children. A spasm of agony struck his heart, for he knew well enough the dangers of Cassar's seasonal sandstorms. The three of them had been fortunate to survive, indeed. His gaze returned to Lindsay, who sat with eyes closed not even trying to disguise her exhaustion. Once, long ago, he had let pride cause a rift in his relationship with Yasmin and, though it had been an accident, he had lost her forever. This time, he told himself, his jaw clenched with determination, he would not make the same mistake. And that was a promise—to himself and to Lindsay.

"What about the horses, Karim?" Lindsay asked as she watched him settle beside her.

"The guards will water them and ride them back to the palace in the morning."

What happened after that—the noisy helicopter ride, the doctor's ministrations at the palace, her petulant insistence on having a bath before being put to bed—was all a blurred memory to Lindsay. But she remembered the affection of those who attended her and the blissful feel of the satin sheets as two bronzed hands tucked her in before she fell into a peaceful, tranquilizer-induced sleep.

When consciousness stirred Lindsay it was dark outside and only the soft glow of the bedside lamp threw light about the room. With eyes still closed she stretched beneath the sheet and uttered a soft sigh. She rolled onto her back, and her eyes opened. They widened with surprise as she saw Karim sitting sentinellike by her bed, watching her every move.

"*Massa' 'alkahyr,*" he said. "You are awake at last. I was beginning to think Dr. Farouk had given you too much sedation."

"Good evening," she responded, at once unaccountably shy at finding him in her quarters.

"How do you feel?"

Lindsay thought for a moment, then told him, "Hungry, as a matter of fact, and thirsty."

"Of course." He went to the small kitchen behind the screen and was back in double-quick time with a large jug and a glass of fruit juice, which he handed to her. "The doctor said you must have plenty of fluid because of the slight dehydration. He wanted to hospitalize you and the twins, just for observation, but I wouldn't permit it."

Yes, that sounded like her autocratic sheikh. He would want to have them all where he could keep an eye on them personally. "How... are the twins?" she asked.

"Aaahh, children. Are they not a constant source of amazement? They seem none the worse for their misadventure. They have rested and eaten and generally are enjoying being made a fuss of by everyone."

"Thank God . . .'' she said with feeling and momentarily closed her eyes so he wouldn't see the rush of tears welling there.

"I will order a tray from the kitchen for you, but you must stay in bed till tomorrow. Dr. Farouk has so ordered.'' He gave her a forbidding look in case she planned to disobey. He went to the phone and placed the request with the kitchen staff, then he refilled her glass with more juice and urged her to drink, which she was pleased to do.

"I'll go and hurry the kitchen up personally,'' he decided, retreating to the door. With a single backward glance at her he left the room.

After he'd gone Lindsay tried to relax but she couldn't. It was true that the sandstorm and the long night by the seashore had drained her energy, and she knew she would need some inner strength to cope with the half-expected confrontation with Karim. Although he had said nothing out of place so far, she clearly recalled his taut, unfathomable expression as he had scooped her up in his arms. Its intensity had frightened her into a stunned silence then, and now, not knowing what he intended to say, she was confused and worried.

Eventually she eased herself out of bed and stood up. She had to wait several seconds for the dizziness to subside before making it to the bathroom where she studied her reflection in the full-length mirror. She grimaced at her pallor and her tangled mass of blond hair and, with a sigh, brushed her locks into some kind of order before returning to her room.

She straightened the divan sheet and put more cushions behind the pillows so she could sit up in bed. She was about to climb under the sheet when a familiar, assertive tone assailed her ears.

"What are you doing out of bed? Get into it at once.''

She jumped with fright and guiltily turned in his direction. The sheikh was standing in the open doorway balancing a laden tray with one hand, the other still on the doorknob. Her throat contracted at the sight of him still wearing his desert robes. He looked marvelous. Her senses rejoiced at the quickening of her heart and the corresponding throb at the base of her throat, but she was desperate to hide her body's betrayal.

"Dr. Farouk said you were not to set foot out of bed for twenty-four hours, Lindsay. So, just this once, will you please do what you're told?"

"Yes, Excellency." And with a meekness that surprised her she dived, with what grace she could find, beneath the covers.

After she had settled herself he set the tea tray across her lap and lifted the covers one by one. "What has Tima prepared for you, I wonder? Aahh yes, *mulookhiyyah* and *taboolih* and for dessert *kul washkur.*"

Lindsay looked at the stew, parsley salad and mouthwatering pastries, but the hunger that had so recently gnawed at her empty stomach had dissolved—evaporated by the tightly composed, emotionless mask of Karim's face. "I'm not hungry now," she told him.

"Ridiculous. You were starving ten minutes ago and you will eat and drink something," he said sternly. He looked at her tense expression, the hint of distress in her glorious green eyes, and the feelings he'd been holding in for more than twelve hours began to scream for release. She had caused him more anxiety and greater fear than any female was worth, his Arabian logic told him. But . . . he loved her with a desperation that was becoming more apparent to him as each moment in her company passed, and such feelings negated every other consideration, good or otherwise. She was safe now; her courage and her quick thinking had probably saved all of them, and for that he would be eternally grateful. What he really wanted to do, he secretly thrilled to the admission, was to hold her close to his heart and kiss her fears away, as he had done with his daughter. But not yet.

"I . . . can't . . ." she muttered softly, embarrassingly on the verge of tears.

"You can and you will," he assured her in a more gentle tone. "Dr. Farouk says you must, to regain your strength."

Once she would have debated the point with him but momentarily she was no match for his will. Grudgingly she picked up a fork and began to push the stew of vegetables and chicken and rice around the plate.

But Karim, after watching for a few moments, clucked his tongue impatiently and threatened, "Would you like me to spoon-feed you like a child? I will, if you don't start to eat something soon, Lindsay."

She gave him a rebellious look. Then, with her spirit stung by his derisive tone, she muttered with what haughtiness she could muster, "I just don't care to be watched while I eat, thank you."

"So be it." He shrugged his shoulders in apparent indifference and strode to the window. He opened the drapes and tried to appear greatly taken with the nighttime view of the floodlit garden and the city skyline beyond. But in reality he was wondering how to go about getting through to her. Telling her of his love for her. She had built up a defensive wall around herself because she thought their differing backgrounds were insurmountable objects. It was a problem, he confessed, but was he not an extraordinarily good diplomat skilled at solving all kinds of problems, political and otherwise? Yes, there had to be a way....

Lindsay began to eat and found, after a few mouthfuls, that her appetite had returned. She ate most of the stew and a few bites of the sweet, multilayered pastries, enough to satisfy even him, before pushing the tray to the foot of the divan.

When he turned to face her again and saw the half-empty tray he smiled with satisfaction. "Good. I am sure you will feel much better after that meal."

Because she did and because she wanted to bring an end to the invisible veil of tension between them, she said straight out, "I'm really sorry for what happened, Karim. I had no idea that the twins would take it into their heads to go exploring while I was at the souk. And the sandstorm... perhaps I should have seen it coming sooner."

"And how would you? You are not a native of this country. You wouldn't know what to look for."

"True, but the risk to their young lives.... If anything had happened to them, I—"

"And what about your life, Lindsay? That was at risk, too," he pointed out as he closed the distance between the window and the wide divan and sat in the chair beside it.

She shook her head as she studied his hawkish, noble features, and what little confidence she'd bolstered herself up with deserted her. "My life's not so important... but Sonja's and Darius's? If..." Her eyes began to mist, and she couldn't say the thoughts out loud. "I'd never forgive myself..." But suddenly overcome by the mental image of how differently things might have turned out, her strength failed and she covered her face with her hands. It was too awful to contemplate. It hadn't happened, but when she recalled how close to death all of them had been, reaction and relief set in in earnest, and she began to tremble uncontrollably.

"Lindsay...please..." The breaking of her self-control shocked him, and momentarily he was at a loss to know how to console her. "You... must stop this," he murmured tenderly, then, knowing of no other way, he sat on the side of the divan and gathered her in his arms and just let her sob it out of her system. Stroking her blond, wavy hair with his bronzed hand he whispered reassuringly to her that everything was all right.

After a long time his words sank in and, pulling slightly back from him, she said in a tone echoing amazement "You're not angry over what happened?" After a teary sniff she added, "For what almost happened?"

The anger, born of fear, that he'd felt earlier melted beneath the flame of love he had for this maddening, independent, courageous woman. "Not anymore," he said simply. His anger had been mostly self-directed anyway, not at her. And she was so lovely and soft and quite adorable. His throat tightened. "Especially if you promise to stop those tears. I—" he paused "—find them most disconcerting." He took a folded handkerchief from his robe and tenderly wiped the tears from her cheeks.

His sudden gentleness and concerned tone quite astonished her. She'd been sure he would somehow take her to task for allowing such a thing to happen. But then she remembered he was a just man and knew where the blame really lay. "About the twins, Karim. You are not going to punish them too severely, are you? I think the fright they've had will teach them a greater lesson than any punishment you could devise."

"You could be right. I will think about it some more before deciding. They are enjoying a little pampering right now, especially Sonja. Ali and Hisham both are catering to her every whim."

"Good for her," Lindsay said decisively, "a little spoiling won't do her any harm. Especially from those undersized chauvinists."

His black eyes fastened on her, studying her with a raw intensity, and one bushy eyebrow rose in question. "You... would enjoy such pampering too, I suppose?" Without waiting for her reply he removed the tray from the divan and began to plump up the cushions behind her and generally fuss over the neatness of the satin sheet covering her.

Such attention made her aware of her skimpy cotton nightie, and her body began to throb, love for him quickening to desire. "I d-don't need to be fussed over...." she assured him as she grabbed the edge of the sheet from him. "Please, don't..." Of course he feigned innocence, but she guessed he knew the inner furor his attention caused her, the wretch!

And suddenly it came to him how he might best broach the subject closest to his heart. "But I must take care of you, Lindsay. Good care. The emir has decreed that ...take a bride...and you're..."

"I know," she interrupted, gloom setting in as her heart plummeted to the lowest depths imaginable. "He said as much the day he inspected the desalination plant."

"Did he now?" The sheikh's remark came out softly, contemplatively. "I'll wager he never hinted at who she might be, though?"

"No." Then she took what courage she had and ventured forth the hateful question. "Who?"

"You, Lindsay. The emir wants us to wed."

The room tilted to an odd angle for several seconds, then righted itself. As the dizziness in her head receded she croaked, "Me! Why? I...don't...understand...I assumed he'd choose someone of your own race." Her mind was doing mental flip-flops trying to come to terms, to understand what this might mean....

"The emir thinks we're well suited in spite of the surface differences." And with an eyebrow raised in challenge, he added, "He doesn't seem to think the fact that we come from vastly different worlds is a problem at all."

Lindsay's eyes widened hugely, and her forehead creased with consternation. "He doesn't?" She didn't know what to make of the emir's astonishing decree or the obvious evidence before her of Karim's complacency. When she looked closely at him again and saw something in his eyes that he couldn't quite disguise, hope began to blossom.

"He doesn't," he repeated firmly, the ghost of a smile playing about his strong, sensitive mouth.

From beneath her fair lashes she took another sly, upward glance at the man she loved quite desperately, and slowly the words she wanted to say formed in her mind. But dare she utter them? She must. Taking a deep breath, she said, "If I knew that you wanted to, and not because the emir had ordered it . . ."

"I do want it, Lindsay, very much, and my desire has nothing to do with my ruler's request," he said, his voice husky with passion.

"Oh." She swallowed hard and lifted her face to his; they were only inches apart now. "Then m-my answer would be . . . is . . . yes."

There was a sharp intake of breath from Karim, and something wonderful shone in his eyes. But still he doubted the message his ears had heard and asked, "And what has brought about this change of heart? You had strong doubts, Lindsay. Such fears! I recall them well. . . ."

"I know," she whispered, "I was—they were—stupid." She saw his skeptical gaze on her and hurried on. "I had time to think while you were away with Prince Zoltan, so much time. About what I was afraid of and why. I underestimated the depth of my love for you and thought, foolishly, that I could get over you. But I couldn't, Karim. Every day without you my love grew stronger and as I grew in confidence my fears lessened, until I saw that our happiness depends on us. On what we do. I now believe that we can whittle the differences down till they disappear completely."

"Oh, Lindsay, darling. How I love you. I never thought I'd hear you admit to your feelings, though. I almost despaired of it happening, just as I knew that nothing I said would convince you. You had to arrive at the conclusion yourself."

"I did—several weeks ago, in fact," she shyly admitted to him.

"Why didn't you say something when you returned from the Riviera? You acted as if what we'd found at the Remarkable Cave was just a dream," he said reproachfully. But even as he said it his arms were closing about her, drawing her to him.

She looked up at him lovingly, her hands moving to twine around his neck, now bold enough to reveal her love. "Because you seemed distant, as if you'd lost interest."

He groaned. "I was trying to be patient. Trying to give you time to see how much alike, rather than different, we really are. Perhaps..." His arms tightened possessively about her, and he again vowed silently that he would never let Lindsay Pentecost go. "I should not have waited so long to..."

He captured her face in his hands and looked deeply into her eyes for a very long time. Then his gaze moved to fasten on her lips, which parted expectantly, and with a moan he brought his mouth down on hers in a sizzling, demanding kiss of triumph. Her wholehearted response left him in no doubt as to her feelings. Needing to have her closer, he threw back the sheet and maneuvered her body till she was sitting in his lap.

"I'm sorry I've been foolish," she confessed. "Forgive me?"

"Hmmm..." he muttered, his features sobering as he appeared to give her request consideration. "You'll have to earn my forgiveness, woman." His eyes glittered darkly with anticipation. "Starting on our wedding night." He grinned at her blush, then kissed her with such hunger that, when he finally released her, she trembled in his arms. "My only regret, my love, is that it has taken so long to reach a...satisfactory conclusion. You...will marry me, soon?"

"The sooner the better." She smiled dreamily, deeply, into his eyes, secretly reveling in the love she planned to lavish on him for the rest of their lives. And then she thought of something and frowned. "The children, Karim—do you think they will approve of our marriage?"

His answer was both immediate and confident. "Of course. As will the majority of the people of Cassar, and particularly the emir. The old rogue has a rather soft spot for you, I think, and will no doubt congratulate himself on such a fine matchmaking task." She smiled charmingly at him and the urge to kiss her again was irresistible. He surrendered to it, and they spent several breathless moments absorbed in each other. Then, breaking away from her, he took a deep, calming breath and said decisively, "I could organize our wedding tomorrow evening. The French priest down at the oil refinery would be pleased to perform the ceremony."

"Sounds wonderful," she happily agreed, her accelerated heartbeat and the intoxicating pulsing through her veins confirming that she couldn't wait to be his.

"No, that's too soon," he said. "We'd better make it the day after to give you extra time to regain your health. And if you desire it, would you like your mother and half sister, Blaise, to attend? I could have the emir's jet fly them here."

Lindsay's eyes sparkled with delight at both his generosity and his thoughtfulness. "Yes, that would be wonderful . . . and could David, my stepfather come, too?" she asked.

"Of course, my love. He can give the bride away," he said with a loving, indulgent smile. "And after the ceremony where would you like to honeymoon?"

A delightful shade of pink suffused her cheeks once more and unconsciously her fingers began to stroke the back of his neck. "I don't care where. Anywhere that's very private would be perfect."

He recognized a yearning that matched his own, and his returning smile showed he was pleased with her reply. "I know of such a place—an island in the South Pacific. No phones, no people, just the two of us."

"Really?" An eyebrow rose in teasing disbelief. "No children, no servants, no demanding emir?"

He stopped her with a kiss and then whispered against her lips. "No distractions whatsoever," he promised.

"Sounds like paradise," she whispered back. And it would be with Karim El Hareembi, her sheikh.

A frown creased his forehead as he thought of something and he asked, "But who will cook for us?"

She gave him a radiant smile, the light in her green eyes luminous with love. "I can cook. That is if we find we get hungry . . . for food."

"I have a ravenous appetite," he admitted with a huskiness that told her he was thinking of an entirely different kind of sustenance, "for you, my dearest, unto eternity," he vowed. Threading his hands through her blond hair, he gently tugged and brought her eager lips to his.

* * *

Neither Lindsay nor Karim heard the quiet tap on the door of her quarters nor saw Darius's curly topped head swivel through the opening. The boy's dark eyes rounded hugely at the picture of his father embracing his tutor, and a puzzled frown puckered his young forehead.

For perhaps twenty seconds he watched the adults' absorption in each other, and then the frown disappeared, replaced by a look of comprehension. He gave a nod of approval, soundlessly shut the door and walked away whistling. . . .

* * * * *

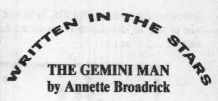

WRITTEN IN THE STARS

THE GEMINI MAN
by Annette Broadrick

Agent: Joel Kramer—gallant Gemini, man of mystery.

Assignment: Secretly protect damsel in distress at a *close* distance.

For undercover agent Joel Kramer, masquerading as the friendly neighbor of a lonely, lovely biochemist promised to be sexy surveillance work. Especially since he planned to teach Melissa Jordan what chemistry really meant....

Look for THE GEMINI MAN by Annette Broadrick in June...the sixth book in our Written in the Stars series!

Silhouette Romance ®

IT'S A CELEBRATION OF MOTHERHOOD!

Following the success of BIRDS, BEES and BABIES, we are proud to announce our second collection of Mother's Day stories.

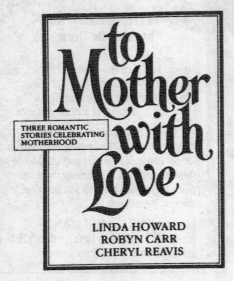

to
Mother
with
Love

THREE ROMANTIC
STORIES CELEBRATING
MOTHERHOOD

LINDA HOWARD
ROBYN CARR
CHERYL REAVIS

Three stories in one volume, all by award-winning authors—stories especially selected to reflect the love all families share.

Available in May, TO MOTHER WITH LOVE is a perfect gift for yourself or a loved one to celebrate the joy of motherhood.

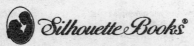 *Silhouette Books*®

ML-1

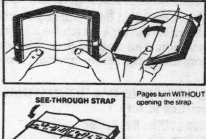

Bestselling author **NORA ROBERTS** captures all the
romance, adventure, passion and excitement of Silhouette in
a special miniseries.

THE CALHOUN WOMEN

Four charming, beautiful and fiercely independent
sisters set out on a search for a missing family
heirloom—an emerald necklace—and each finds
something even more precious...passionate romance.

Look for THE CALHOUN WOMEN miniseries
starting in June.

COURTING CATHERINE
Silhouette Romance #801

July
A MAN FOR AMANDA
Silhouette Desire #649

August
FOR THE LOVE OF LILAH
Silhouette Special Edition #685

September
SUZANNA'S SURRENDER
Silhouette Intimate Moments #397

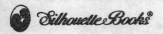 *Silhouette Books®*

CALWOM-1